WEIGHT WATCHERS®

1990

ENGAGEMENT CALENDAR

NAL BOOKS

NEW AMERICAN LIBRARY

A DIVISION OF PENGUIN BOOKS USA INC., NEW YORK

PUBLISHED IN CANADA BY
PENGUIN BOOKS CANADA LIMITED, MARKHAM, ONTARIO

WEIGHT WATCHERS is a registered trademark of
Weight Watchers International, Inc.

NAL BOOKS TRADEMARK REG. U.S. PAT. OFF. AND FOREIGN COUNTRIES
REGISTERED TRADEMARK—MARCA REGISTRADA
HECHO EN HARRISONBURG, VA., U.S.A.

SIGNET, SIGNET CLASSIC, MENTOR, ONYX, PLUME, MERIDIAN and
NAL BOOKS are published *in the United States* by New American Library,
a division of Penguin Books USA Inc., 1633 Broadway, New York,
New York 10019, *in Canada* by Penguin Books Canada Limited, 2801
John Street, Markham, Ontario L3R 1B4

Designed by John Lynch

Cover photo by Gus Francisco

Weight Watchers is a registered trademark of
Weight Watchers International, Inc.

First Printing, August, 1989

1 2 3 4 5 6 7 8 9

PRINTED IN THE UNITED STATES OF AMERICA

Welcome to a brand-new decade! Over the years, we've responded to your requests for quick, easy, and nutritious recipes by bringing you our best-selling cookbooks and engagement calendars. Now, the WEIGHT WATCHERS 1990 ENGAGEMENT CALENDAR presents a new collection of some of the quickest and easiest recipes ever, thanks to the magic of microwave cooking.

Each month we present four tempting microwave recipes, 48 in all, that can also be prepared in a conventional oven or on the range. You'll find such holiday dishes as Acorn Squash and Cheddar Gratin (November) and Raspberry Pudding Pie (February). Enjoy Irish Bread Pudding on St. Patrick's Day; make Matzo Torte for Passover; serve Corn on the Cob with Lemon-Chive Butter at your Fourth of July barbecue. There are so many delicious dishes, you're sure to find a favorite among them. And if it's menu ideas you're looking for, don't miss our Microwave Menu of the Month—each one features a highlighted recipe from that month's dishes.

Our Engagement Calendar also features two special sections chock-full of information on how to get the best results from your microwave oven as well as from our recipes. The Calendar also contains a practical Weekly Food Diary to help you plan your meals, keep track of your Daily Totals and Weekly Limits, and even remind yourself of your weekly Weight Watchers meeting. And there's plenty of room on the weekly and monthly calendar pages to record appointments, birthdays, anniversaries, and all the other important events in your busy life.

We hope you enjoy using the WEIGHT WATCHERS 1990 ENGAGEMENT CALENDAR, and may you and your microwave oven produce many memorable meals together!

Successful Microwave Cooking

If ever an appliance deserved an award for popularity, the microwave oven is it. Now almost as commonplace as televisions and stereo systems, microwave ovens are no longer the "big ticket" items they once were. Two thirds of all households own one, and that number is expected to rise to more than 90 percent during this decade. Increasingly popular are the compact ovens that take up less counter space, as well as those that can be mounted under kitchen cabinets.

Unfortunately, many people don't realize all of the advantages of a microwave, and they buy one only for heating leftovers and defrosting frozen foods. But the microwave oven offers much more in the way of convenience.

• With the microwave, cooking time is short, and little or no water is needed. That means foods retain the vitamins and minerals that normally leach out into the cooking liquid and are discarded. Foods with a high water content, such as soups, most vegetables, fruits, and fish, are particularly good cooked in the microwave oven.

• The microwave is energy-efficient. It cooks food in less time than a conventional oven and consequently uses less energy, making it less expensive to operate.

• With a microwave, foods can be served in the same utensil they are cooked in. For an easy snack, heat soup in a microwavable mug or soup bowl rather than a saucepan. When heating up leftovers, arrange the entire meal attractively on a microwavable dinner plate with thick foods on the outside of the plate and those foods that heat more easily in the center, for a fast one-dish meal.

• Microwave cooking requires less margarine, butter, and oil—you need use only enough for flavoring.

• The microwave oven cavity remains cool, which means spills and spatters do not "bake on." The oven interior can be wiped clean with a damp sponge or cloth.

• Microwave cooking is safer than conventional cooking because there are no hot surfaces inside or outside the oven. Older children can prepare after-school snacks in the microwave without the danger of getting burned. Remember to use pot holders because cookware can become warm.

• A mobile appliance, the microwave oven can be moved around easily and needs no special installation.

The Microwave Ovens We Used

The wattage of a microwave oven is its total cooking power. Ovens vary from 400 watts (compact ovens) to 750 watts (full-size ovens). The recipes in this book were tested in 650- to 700-watt microwave ovens. If you own a lower wattage oven, you can still count on terrific results if you increase the cooking time slightly, check for doneness, and then cook longer if necessary. If you're using a higher wattage oven, you'll need to decrease the cooking time slightly.

Our recipes were tested in ovens that had variable power levels. Power levels control the percentage of power introduced into the oven cavity and automatically cycle the power on and off. Higher power levels cook food faster and lower power levels cook food more slowly. The following are the power levels in the ovens we used:

High (100%)
Medium-High (60–70%)
Medium (50%)
Medium-Low (30%)
Low (10–20%)

Since power varies depending on the brand of oven, the cooking time may need to be adjusted depending on your oven's power level.

Microwave Cooking Techniques

You'll get the best results from your microwave oven if you use the following techniques.

Stirring—For range-top cooking, stirring usually serves to prevent food from scorching, but for microwave cooking, food is stirred to redistribute heat. Many of our recipes indicate when stirring is necessary.

Rearranging—Because the corners or sides of a cooking utensil receive more energy than the center, it is necessary during the cooking time to rearrange foods that can't be stirred.

Rotating or Turning—Rotating is necessary when a food cannot be stirred or rearranged. This is done by moving the cooking utensil a half or quarter turn. Cakes, pies, muffins, and some casseroles require rotating during cooking.

Piercing—Piercing the skin or outer membrane of foods such as winter squash, eggplant, potatoes, egg yolks, and chicken livers keeps them from bursting due to steam buildup during cooking. You can pierce food with a sharp paring knife or the tines of a fork. And remember, *never* microwave eggs in the shell: If you do, they'll explode and you'll have quite a mess to clean up.

Standing Time—You may notice that some of our recipes indicate standing time. These few extra minutes allow for a completion of cooking in the center or in thicker areas of the food.

Microwave Oven Accessories

• Battery-operated or spring-wound *turntables* can be placed on the floor of your microwave oven. The cookware or food is placed on the turntable, which rotates as the food cooks. With a turntable, foods cook more evenly and there is no need to stop the cooking process and rotate the food or dish manually.

• *Browning trays*, which are available in numerous shapes and sizes, are used to sear, brown, or crisp foods. This specially coated tray is first placed in the microwave oven and preheated to absorb microwave energy and become very hot. Browning occurs when the food is placed on the preheated dish and microwaved.

• Many microwave ovens are equipped with a built-in *probe* that is used to determine doneness. If your oven isn't equipped with a probe, you may want to invest in a microwave thermometer. (Conventional thermometers cannot be used in the microwave oven.)

Microwave Oven Cookware

You don't need a complete set of new cooking utensils to cook in a microwave oven. Many utensils that you already own can be used and some new utensils currently on the market can be used in both a conventional oven and a microwave.

In general, ovenproof glass, ceramic, and pottery dishes that have no metallic trim can safely be used in the microwave. In fact, many dishes now can go from freezer to microwave to table. Some plastics can be used in the microwave. However, it's a good idea to check the manufacturers' recommendations since certain kinds of plastic may melt, especially if used with foods high in fat or sugar, which become very hot when cooked.

Metal and Your Microwave

With the exception of aluminum foil, metal should not be used in the microwave oven. Metal reflects microwaves away from the food rather than allowing them to pass through to cook. Aluminum foil, however, is helpful because it can shield areas that begin to overcook. When thawing frozen foods, you can use foil to protect already thawed outer edges which may begin to cook before the center of the meat is fully thawed. Covering these spots with small pieces of aluminum foil protects them. Be sure not to allow the foil to come in contact with the oven walls as this can damage the oven.

Is Your Cookware Microwave-Safe?

It's a good idea to test the cookware you already own to see if it is safe to use in the microwave. To do this, place the utensil in the oven along with

—but not touching—a 1-cup glass measure filled with ½ cup of cool water. (The water absorbs microwaves and prevents damage to your oven.) Microwave on High (100%) for 1 minute. The utensil should be cool or slightly warm to the touch. If it is hot, it is not safe for use in the microwave.

How to Cover While You Cook

The matching covers that accompany your microwave cookware can be used to cover food as you cook. The following paper products are also commonly used as covers.

Wax Paper—Covering a dish with wax paper holds in heat, speeds the cooking process, and prevents spatters.

Plastic Wrap—It's important to purchase plastic wrap that is labeled "For Microwave Use," as other brands of wrap may melt during cooking. Plastic wrap forms a tight cover that keeps in moisture. However, the seal can be so tight that excess steam builds up and will burn you when you remove the wrap. For this reason, when you cover the dish, fold back a corner of the plastic wrap to allow excess steam to escape; this technique is called venting. If a recipe does require that you *tightly* cover a dish with plastic wrap, you will need to pierce the plastic with a knife, and then carefully remove the plastic in a direction away from you to avoid a burn.

Paper Towels—Paper towels approved for microwave usage not only allow steam to escape and reduce spattering but also absorb moisture.

Eliminating Odors in Your Microwave Oven

To avoid unpleasant odors, be sure to wipe up spatters from the interior surface of the oven as soon as possible, or the food particles will become spoiled and rancid. Some foods, such as cabbage and highly seasoned foods, can also cause odors. You can remove these odors by combining ½ cup lemon juice and 1 cup water in a large microwavable glass and letting the mixture boil in the microwave for several minutes. Let stand for 5 to 6 minutes before removing.

How to Use the Recipes

The recipes in this Engagement Calendar can be prepared in the microwave oven, as well as in a conventional oven or on the range. Since we give the method for both microwave and conventional cooking, it's important to read the recipe carefully and assemble all the necessary ingredients before you begin.

We also recommend that you read the instructions that came with your microwave oven, as not all models are alike.

JANUARY

SUNDAY	MONDAY	TUESDAY	WEDNESDAY
	1	2 Dr Lawrence 4:30	3
7	8	9	10
14	15	16	17
21	22	23	24
28	29	30	31

THURSDAY	FRIDAY	SATURDAY
4	5	6
11	12	13
18	19	20
25	26	27

Microwave Menu of the Month

Deviled Crab and Cheese Hors d'Oeuvres

Clove-Studded Baked Virginia Ham

Baked Sweet Potato with Margarine

Cooked Green Beans

Red Leaf Lettuce and Sprout Salad with Roquefort Dressing

Lemon Sorbet

Champagne

NOTES/GOALS

WEEKLY FOOD DIARY

DAILY TOTALS	MONDAY	TUESDAY	WEDNESDAY	THURSDAY	FRIDAY	SATURDAY	SUNDAY
FRUIT ___ VEG ___ FAT ___ PROTEIN ___ BREAD ___ MILK ___ FLOATING ___						FRUIT ___ VEG ___ FAT ___ PROTEIN ___ BREAD ___ MILK ___ FLOATING ___	FRUIT ___ VEG ___ FAT ___ PROTEIN ___ BREAD ___ MILK ___ FLOATING ___
BREAKFAST	Cereal & milk 5.4	Egg E.muffin 10.1	Cereal & milk Banana				
LUNCH	Sw-CBeef / Cheese 1/2 Apple 25.0	Sw.w/Ham 1/2 Apple 4.7	Sw-Ham / Cheese Apple Fruitcake				
DINNER	Cauliflower G.Beans 0.6 Total 31	Roast-w veys 6.Crackers w/Butter	Cereal & milk Banana Egg&Emuffin				
SNACKS	6 Total 37	Total 36.4	Total 35				

WEEKLY LIMITS ___ EGGS ___ MEAT ___ ORGAN MEAT ___ OPTIONAL CALORIES ___

CHEESE ___

I will attend my Weight Watchers meeting this week on ___

JANUARY

1 9 9 0

New Year's Day 1990

MONDAY
1

Beverly Called

TUESDAY
2

WEDNESDAY
3

THURSDAY
4

'**FRIDAY**
5

SATURDAY
6

SUNDAY
7

	S	M	T	W	T	F	S
D E C						1	2
	3	4	5	6	7	8	9
	10	11	12	13	14	15	16
	17	18	19	20	21	22	23
	24	25	26	27	28	29	30
	31						

	S	M	T	W	T	F	S
J A N		1	2	3	4	5	6
	7	8	9	10	11	12	13
	14	15	16	17	18	19	20
	21	22	23	24	25	26	27
	28	29	30	31			

	S	M	T	W	T	F	S
F E B					1	2	3
	4	5	6	7	8	9	10
	11	12	13	14	15	16	17
	18	19	20	21	22	23	24
	25	26	27	28			

WEEKLY FOOD DIARY

	MONDAY	TUESDAY	WEDNESDAY	THURSDAY	FRIDAY	SATURDAY	SUNDAY
DAILY TOTALS	FRUIT ___ VEG ___ FAT ___ PROTEIN ___ BREAD ___ MILK ___ FLOATING ___		FRUIT ___ VEG ___ FAT ___ PROTEIN ___ BREAD ___ MILK ___ FLOATING ___	FRUIT ___ VEG ___ FAT ___ PROTEIN ___ BREAD ___ MILK ___ FLOATING ___	FRUIT ___ VEG ___ FAT ___ PROTEIN ___ BREAD ___ MILK ___ FLOATING ___	FRUIT ___ VEG ___ FAT ___ PROTEIN ___ BREAD ___ MILK ___ FLOATING ___	FRUIT ___ VEG ___ FAT ___ PROTEIN ___ BREAD ___ MILK ___ FLOATING ___
BREAKFAST							
LUNCH							
DINNER							
SNACKS							

WEEKLY LIMITS   EGGS _____   CHEESE _____   MEAT _____   ORGAN MEAT _____   OPTIONAL CALORIES _____

I will attend my Weight Watchers meeting this week on _____

MONDAY
8

TUESDAY
9

WEDNESDAY
10

THURSDAY
11

FRIDAY
12

SATURDAY
13

SUNDAY
14

	S	M	T	W	T	F	S
							1	2
D	3	4	5	6	7	8	9
E	10	11	12	13	14	15	16
C	17	18	19	20	21	22	23
	24	25	26	27	28	29	30
	31						

	S	M	T	W	T	F	S
		1	2	3	4	5	6
J	7	8	9	10	11	12	13
A	14	15	16	17	18	19	20
N	21	22	23	24	25	26	27
	28	29	30	31			

	S	M	T	W	T	F	S
					1	2	3
F	4	5	6	7	8	9	10
E	11	12	13	14	15	16	17
B	18	19	20	21	22	23	24
	25	26	27	28			

WEEKLY FOOD DIARY

	MONDAY	TUESDAY	WEDNESDAY	THURSDAY	FRIDAY	SATURDAY	SUNDAY
DAILY TOTALS	FRUIT ___ VEG ___ FAT ___ PROTEIN ___ BREAD ___ MILK ___ FLOATING ___	FRUIT ___ VEG ___ FAT ___ PROTEIN ___ BREAD ___ MILK ___ FLOATING ___	FRUIT ___ VEG ___ FAT ___ PROTEIN ___ BREAD ___ MILK ___ FLOATING ___	FRUIT ___ VEG ___ FAT ___ PROTEIN ___ BREAD ___ MILK ___ FLOATING ___	FRUIT ___ VEG ___ FAT ___ PROTEIN ___ BREAD ___ MILK ___ FLOATING ___	FRUIT ___ VEG ___ FAT ___ PROTEIN ___ BREAD ___ MILK ___ FLOATING ___	FRUIT ___ VEG ___ FAT ___ PROTEIN ___ BREAD ___ MILK ___ FLOATING ___
BREAKFAST							
LUNCH							
DINNER							
SNACKS							

WEEKLY LIMITS   EGGS ___   CHEESE ___   MEAT ___   ORGAN MEAT ___   OPTIONAL CALORIES ___

I will attend my Weight Watchers meeting this week on ___

Martin Luther King, Jr.'s Birthday

MONDAY
15

TUESDAY
16

WEDNESDAY
17

THURSDAY
18

FRIDAY
19

SATURDAY
20

SUNDAY
21

	S	M	T	W	T	F	S
						1	2
D	3	4	5	6	7	8	9
E	10	11	12	13	14	15	16
C	17	18	19	20	21	22	23
	24	25	26	27	28	29	30
	31						

	S	M	T	W	T	F	S
		1	2	3	4	5	6
J	7	8	9	10	11	12	13
A	14	15	16	17	18	19	20
N	21	22	23	24	25	26	27
	28	29	30	31			

	S	M	T	W	T	F	S
					1	2	3
F	4	5	6	7	8	9	10
E	11	12	13	14	15	16	17
B	18	19	20	21	22	23	24
	25	26	27	28			

WEEKLY FOOD DIARY

	MONDAY	TUESDAY	WEDNESDAY	THURSDAY	FRIDAY	SATURDAY	SUNDAY
DAILY TOTALS	FRUIT ___ VEG ___ FAT ___ PROTEIN ___ BREAD ___ MILK ___ FLOATING ___	FRUIT ___ VEG ___ FAT ___ PROTEIN ___ BREAD ___ MILK ___ FLOATING ___	FRUIT ___ VEG ___ FAT ___ PROTEIN ___ BREAD ___ MILK ___ FLOATING ___	FRUIT ___ VEG ___ FAT ___ PROTEIN ___ BREAD ___ MILK ___ FLOATING ___	FRUIT ___ VEG ___ FAT ___ PROTEIN ___ BREAD ___ MILK ___ FLOATING ___	FRUIT ___ VEG ___ FAT ___ PROTEIN ___ BREAD ___ MILK ___ FLOATING ___	FRUIT ___ VEG ___ FAT ___ PROTEIN ___ BREAD ___ MILK ___ FLOATING ___
BREAKFAST							
LUNCH							
DINNER							
SNACKS							

WEEKLY LIMITS   EGGS ___   CHEESE ___   MEAT ___   ORGAN MEAT ___   OPTIONAL CALORIES ___

I will attend my Weight Watchers meeting this week on ___

MONDAY
22

TUESDAY
23

WEDNESDAY
24

THURSDAY
25

FRIDAY
26

SATURDAY
27

SUNDAY
28

	S	M	T	W	T	F	S
DEC						1	2
	3	4	5	6	7	8	9
	10	11	12	13	14	15	16
	17	18	19	20	21	22	23
	24	25	26	27	28	29	30
	31						

	S	M	T	W	T	F	S
JAN		1	2	3	4	5	6
	7	8	9	10	11	12	13
	14	15	16	17	18	19	20
	21	22	23	24	25	26	27
	28	29	30	31			

	S	M	T	W	T	F	S
FEB					1	2	3
	4	5	6	7	8	9	10
	11	12	13	14	15	16	17
	18	19	20	21	22	23	24
	25	26	27	28			

Deviled Crab and Cheese Hors d'Oeuvres

Makes 4 servings, 3 hors d'oeuvres each

2 ounces cooked fresh *or* thawed and drained frozen crabmeat, flaked
1 ounce shredded Cheddar cheese, divided
2 tablespoons *each* minced scallion (green onion), green bell pepper, celery, and drained canned pimiento

1 tablespoon plus 1 teaspoon reduced-calorie mayonnaise
1 tablespoon Dijon-style mustard
½ teaspoon Worcestershire sauce
Dash hot sauce
12 unsalted saltines

Microwave Method: In medium mixing bowl combine all ingredients except ½ ounce cheese and the saltines; stir well to thoroughly combine.

Spread $\frac{1}{12}$ of crabmeat mixture (about 1 tablespoonful) onto each saltine; top each with an equal amount of the reserved cheese (about 1 teaspoon). Arrange on microwavable tray and microwave on High (100%) for 1 minute, rotating tray ½ turn halfway through cooking, until cheese is melted and crabmeat mixture is heated through.

Conventional Method: In medium mixing bowl combine all ingredients except ½ ounce cheese and the saltines; stir well to thoroughly combine. Spread $\frac{1}{12}$ of crabmeat mixture (about 1 tablespoonful) onto each saltine; top each with an equal amount of the reserved cheese (about 1 teaspoon). Arrange on nonstick baking sheet and broil 5 to 6 inches from heat source until cheese is melted and crabmeat mixure is heated through, 1 to 2 minutes.

Each serving provides: ¾ Protein Exchange; ½ Bread Exchange; ¼ Vegetable Exchange; ½ Fat Exchange

Per serving: 101 calories; 5 g protein; 5 g fat; 8 g carbohydrate; 82 mg calcium; 316 mg sodium; 23 mg cholesterol; 0.2 g dietary fiber (this figure does not include pimiento and saltines; nutrition analyses not available)

Lentil and Sausage Soup

Makes 4 servings, about 1 cup each

½ cup *each* diced onion, carrot, and celery
2 teaspoons olive *or* vegetable oil
1 garlic clove, minced
1 ounce cooked smoked beef *or* cooked veal sausage link, sliced
¼ cup dry sherry
1 quart water

3¾ ounces sorted uncooked lentils, rinsed
3 packets instant chicken broth and seasoning mix
1 tablespoon chopped fresh parsley
1 bay leaf
Dash pepper

Microwave Method: In 3-quart microwavable casserole combine vegetables, oil, and garlic; stir well to thoroughly combine. Cover with vented plastic wrap and microwave on High (100%) for 2 minutes until vegetables are tender. Add sausage and sherry and stir to combine; microwave on High for 30 seconds. Add remaining ingredients and stir to combine; cover with vented plastic wrap and microwave on High for 15 minutes, stirring once halfway through cooking. Reduce power to Medium-High (60%) and microwave for 15 minutes until lentils are tender, stirring once halfway through cooking. Remove and discard bay leaf.

Conventional Method: In 3-quart saucepan heat oil; add vegetables and garlic and sauté over high heat until vegetables are tender, about 2 minutes. Add sausage and sherry and stir to combine; cook 1 minute longer. Stir in remaining ingredients; partially cover and bring mixture to a boil. Reduce heat to low and let simmer, stirring occasionally, until lentils are tender, 30 to 35 minutes. Remove and discard bay leaf.

Each serving provides: 1½ Protein Exchanges; ¾ Vegetable Exchange; ½ Fat Exchange; 25 Optional Calories

Per serving with smoked beef sausage: 181 calories; 10 g protein; 5 g fat; 22 g carbohydrate; 35 mg calcium; 837 mg sodium; 2 mg cholesterol; 4 g dietary fiber

With veal sausage: 174 calories; 11 g protein; 4 g fat; 22 g carbohydrate; 36 mg calcium; 770 mg sodium; 7 mg cholesterol; 4 g dietary fiber

Chicken Liver Canapés

Makes 4 servings, 3 canapés each

5 ounces chicken livers
¼ cup *each* rinsed and drained capers (reserve 12 capers for garnish) and brandy
1 tablespoon minced onion
1 bay leaf

1 small garlic clove, minced
3 tablespoons whipped cream cheese
⅛ teaspoon salt
Dash *each* white pepper and ground nutmeg
12 melba rounds

Microwave Method: With point of sharp paring knife pierce membranes of chicken livers in several places (otherwise livers may explode while cooking in microwave). In 1-quart microwavable casserole combine chicken livers, capers, brandy, onion, bay leaf, and garlic. Cover and refrigerate overnight or at least 30 minutes.

Vent plastic wrap and microwave on High (100%) for 3½ minutes. Let stand for 2 minutes until livers are brown on the outside but still slightly pink on the inside. Remove cover and let cool slightly. Remove and discard bay leaf. Transfer liver mixture to work bowl of food processor; add cream cheese and seasonings and process until pureed, scraping down sides of container as necessary. Transfer mixture to small bowl; cover and refrigerate until firm, about 1 hour.

To serve, onto each melba round spread an equal amount of liver mixture; top each with 1 reserved caper.

Conventional Method: In medium glass or stainless-steel bowl combine chicken livers, capers, brandy, onion, bay leaf, and garlic. Cover and refrigerate overnight or at least 30 minutes.

Transfer liver mixture to 2-quart saucepan; cook over medium heat, stirring occasionally, until livers are brown on the outside but still slightly pink on the inside, about 10 minutes. Remove from heat and let cool slightly. Remove and discard bay leaf. Transfer liver mixture to work bowl of food processor; add cream cheese and seasonings and process until pureed, scraping down sides of container as necessary. Transfer mixture to small bowl; cover and refrigerate until firm, about 1 hour.

Serve as directed in microwave method.

Each serving provides: 1 Protein Exchange; ½ Bread Exchange; 65 Optional Calories

Per Serving: 145 calories; 8 g protein; 4 g fat; 9 g carbohydrate; 15 mg calcium; 344 mg sodium; 163 mg cholesterol; trace dietary fiber

Chicken Fricassee

Makes 2 servings

1 cup sliced carrots (1½-inch pieces)
½ cup *each* **frozen pearl onions and sliced celery**
1 teaspoon olive *or* **vegetable oil**
1 pound 2 ounces chicken parts, skinned
½ cup canned ready-to-serve chicken broth

2 teaspoons all-purpose flour
1 teaspoon chopped fresh parsley
¼ cup frozen peas
2 tablespoons half-and-half (blend of milk and cream)
Dash white pepper

Microwave Method: In 3-quart microwavable casserole combine carrots, onions, celery, and oil; stir well to thoroughly combine. Cover with vented plastic wrap and microwave on High (100%) for 2 minutes until vegetables are tender. Remove plastic wrap and arrange chicken over vegetables with meaty pieces around edges. Replace vented plastic wrap and microwave on High for 8 minutes, rotating dish ½ turn halfway through cooking.

In 1-cup liquid measure combine broth and flour, stirring until flour is dissolved; stir in parsley. Stir mixture into casserole; add remaining ingredients, cover with vented plastic wrap, and microwave on High until chicken is cooked through and mixture thickens slightly, about 3 mintues.

Conventional Method: In 4-quart saucepan heat oil over high heat; add chicken and cook, turning occasionally, until lightly browned, 3 to 4 minutes. Remove from saucepan and set aside.

In same pan combine carrots, onions, and celery and sauté until vegetables are tender, 2 to 3 minutes. Sprinkle flour over vegetables and stir quickly to combine. Stir in broth, parsley, and pepper; return chicken to pan. Reduce heat to low, cover, and cook, stirring occasionally, until chicken is cooked through, 20 to 25 minutes. Stir in peas and half-and-half and cook until heated through, 2 to 3 minutes.

Each serving provides: 3 Protein Exchanges; ¼ Bread Exchange; 2 Vegetable Exchanges; ½ Fat Exchange; 45 Optional Calories

Per serving: 258 calories; 28 g protein; 8 g fat; 18 g carbohydrate; 82 mg calcium; 421 mg sodium; 85 mg cholesterol; 2 g dietary fiber

FEBRUARY

SUNDAY	MONDAY	TUESDAY	WEDNESDAY
4	5	6	7
11	12	13	14
18	19	20	21
25	26	27	28

FEBRUARY

THURSDAY	FRIDAY	SATURDAY
1	2	3
8	9	10
15	16	17
22	23	24

*Microwave
Menu
of the Month*

**Chilled Mixed Vegetable
Juice with Carrot Stick
Stirrer**

**Paprika-Sprinkled
Broiled Scrod**

Cooked Broccoli Spears

Cherry Tomato,
Mushroom, and Romaine
Salad with French
Dressing

Raspberry Pudding Pie

Coffee or Tea

NOTES/GOALS

WEEKLY FOOD DIARY

	MONDAY	TUESDAY	WEDNESDAY	THURSDAY	FRIDAY	SATURDAY	SUNDAY
D A I L Y T O T A L S	FRUIT ____ VEG ____ FAT ____ PROTEIN ____ BREAD ____ MILK ____ FLOATING ____	FRUIT ____ VEG ____ FAT ____ PROTEIN ____ BREAD ____ MILK ____ FLOATING ____	FRUIT ____ VEG ____ FAT ____ PROTEIN ____ BREAD ____ MILK ____ FLOATING ____	FRUIT ____ VEG ____ FAT ____ PROTEIN ____ BREAD ____ MILK ____ FLOATING ____	FRUIT ____ VEG ____ FAT ____ PROTEIN ____ BREAD ____ MILK ____ FLOATING ____	FRUIT ____ VEG ____ FAT ____ PROTEIN ____ BREAD ____ MILK ____ FLOATING ____	FRUIT ____ VEG ____ FAT ____ PROTEIN ____ BREAD ____ MILK ____ FLOATING ____
BREAKFAST							
LUNCH							
DINNER							
SNACKS							

WEEKLY LIMITS   EGGS ____   CHEESE ____   MEAT ____   ORGAN MEAT ____   OPTIONAL CALORIES ____

I will attend my Weight Watchers meeting this week on _____

MONDAY
29

TUESDAY
30

WEDNESDAY
31

THURSDAY
1

FRIDAY
2

SATURDAY
3

SUNDAY
4

	S	M	T	W	T	F	S
		1	2	3	4	5	6
J	7	8	9	10	11	12	13
A	14	15	16	17	18	19	20
N	21	22	23	24	25	26	27
	28	29	30	31			

	S	M	T	W	T	F	S
					1	2	3
F	4	5	6	7	8	9	10
E	11	12	13	14	15	16	17
B	18	19	20	21	22	23	24
	25	26	27	28			

	S	M	T	W	T	F	S
					1	2	3
M	4	5	6	7	8	9	10
A	11	12	13	14	15	16	17
R	18	19	20	21	22	23	24
	25	26	27	28	29	30	31

WEEKLY FOOD DIARY

	MONDAY	TUESDAY	WEDNESDAY	THURSDAY	FRIDAY	SATURDAY	SUNDAY
DAILY TOTALS	FRUIT ___ VEG ___ FAT ___ PROTEIN ___ BREAD ___ MILK ___ FLOATING ___	FRUIT ___ VEG ___ FAT ___ PROTEIN ___ BREAD ___ MILK ___ FLOATING ___	FRUIT ___ VEG ___ FAT ___ PROTEIN ___ BREAD ___ MILK ___ FLOATING ___	FRUIT ___ VEG ___ FAT ___ PROTEIN ___ BREAD ___ MILK ___ FLOATING ___	FRUIT ___ VEG ___ FAT ___ PROTEIN ___ BREAD ___ MILK ___ FLOATING ___	FRUIT ___ VEG ___ FAT ___ PROTEIN ___ BREAD ___ MILK ___ FLOATING ___	FRUIT ___ VEG ___ FAT ___ PROTEIN ___ BREAD ___ MILK ___ FLOATING ___
BREAKFAST							
LUNCH							
DINNER							
SNACKS							

WEEKLY LIMITS EGGS _____ CHEESE _____ MEAT _____ ORGAN MEAT _____ OPTIONAL CALORIES _____

I will attend my Weight Watchers meeting this week on _____

FEBRUARY

1 9 9 0

MONDAY
5

TUESDAY
6

WEDNESDAY
7

THURSDAY
8

FRIDAY
9

SATURDAY
10

SUNDAY
11

	S	M	T	W	T	F	S
		1	2	3	4	5	6
J	7	8	9	10	11	12	13
A	14	15	16	17	18	19	20
N	21	22	23	24	25	26	27
	28	29	30	31			

	S	M	T	W	T	F	S
					1	2	3
F	4	5	6	7	8	9	10
E	11	12	13	14	15	16	17
B	18	19	20	21	22	23	24
	25	26	27	28			

	S	M	T	W	T	F	S
					1	2	3
M	4	5	6	7	8	9	10
A	11	12	13	14	15	16	17
R	18	19	20	21	22	23	24
	25	26	27	28	29	30	31

WEEKLY FOOD DIARY

	MONDAY	TUESDAY	WEDNESDAY	THURSDAY	FRIDAY	SATURDAY	SUNDAY
D A I L Y T O T A L S	FRUIT _____ VEG _____ FAT _____ PROTEIN _____ BREAD _____ MILK _____ FLOATING _____	FRUIT _____ VEG _____ FAT _____ PROTEIN _____ BREAD _____ MILK _____ FLOATING _____	FRUIT _____ VEG _____ FAT _____ PROTEIN _____ BREAD _____ MILK _____ FLOATING _____	FRUIT _____ VEG _____ FAT _____ PROTEIN _____ BREAD _____ MILK _____ FLOATING _____	FRUIT _____ VEG _____ FAT _____ PROTEIN _____ BREAD _____ MILK _____ FLOATING _____	FRUIT _____ VEG _____ FAT _____ PROTEIN _____ BREAD _____ MILK _____ FLOATING _____	FRUIT _____ VEG _____ FAT _____ PROTEIN _____ BREAD _____ MILK _____ FLOATING _____
B R E A K F A S T							
L U N C H							
D I N N E R							
S N A C K S							

WEEKLY LIMITS EGGS _____ CHEESE _____ MEAT _____ ORGAN MEAT _____ OPTIONAL CALORIES _____

I will attend my Weight Watchers meeting this week on _____

ENGAGEMENTS

FEBRUARY

1 9 9 0

Lincoln's Birthday

MONDAY
12

TUESDAY
13

Valentine's Day

WEDNESDAY
14

THURSDAY
15

FRIDAY
16

SATURDAY
17

SUNDAY
18

	S	M	T	W	T	F	S
		1	2	3	4	5	6
J	7	8	9	10	11	12	13
A	14	15	16	17	18	19	20
N	21	22	23	24	25	26	27
	28	29	30	31			

	S	M	T	W	T	F	S
					1	2	3
F	4	5	6	7	8	9	10
E	11	12	13	14	15	16	17
B	18	19	20	21	22	23	24
	25	26	27	28			

	S	M	T	W	T	F	S
					1	2	3
M	4	5	6	7	8	9	10
A	11	12	13	14	15	16	17
R	18	19	20	21	22	23	24
	25	26	27	28	29	30	31

WEEKLY FOOD DIARY

	MONDAY	TUESDAY	WEDNESDAY	THURSDAY	FRIDAY	SATURDAY	SUNDAY
DAILY TOTALS	FRUIT ___ VEG ___ FAT ___ PROTEIN ___ BREAD ___ MILK ___ FLOATING ___	FRUIT ___ VEG ___ FAT ___ PROTEIN ___ BREAD ___ MILK ___ FLOATING ___	FRUIT ___ VEG ___ FAT ___ PROTEIN ___ BREAD ___ MILK ___ FLOATING ___	FRUIT ___ VEG ___ FAT ___ PROTEIN ___ BREAD ___ MILK ___ FLOATING ___	FRUIT ___ VEG ___ FAT ___ PROTEIN ___ BREAD ___ MILK ___ FLOATING ___	FRUIT ___ VEG ___ FAT ___ PROTEIN ___ BREAD ___ MILK ___ FLOATING ___	FRUIT ___ VEG ___ FAT ___ PROTEIN ___ BREAD ___ MILK ___ FLOATING ___
BREAKFAST							
LUNCH							
DINNER							
SNACKS							

WEEKLY LIMITS   EGGS ___   CHEESE ___   MEAT ___   ORGAN MEAT ___   OPTIONAL CALORIES ___

I will attend my Weight Watchers meeting this week on _____

ENGAGEMENTS

FEBRUARY

1990

Washington's Birthday (observed)

MONDAY
19

TUESDAY
20

WEDNESDAY
21

Washington's Birthday

THURSDAY
22

FRIDAY
23

SATURDAY
24

SUNDAY
25

	S	M	T	W	T	F	S
		1	2	3	4	5	6
J	7	8	9	10	11	12	13
A	14	15	16	17	18	19	20
N	21	22	23	24	25	26	27
	28	29	30	31			

	S	M	T	W	T	F	S
					1	2	3
F	4	5	6	7	8	9	10
E	11	12	13	14	15	16	17
B	18	19	20	21	22	23	24
	25	26	27	28			

	S	M	T	W	T	F	S
					1	2	3
M	4	5	6	7	8	9	10
A	11	12	13	14	15	16	17
R	18	19	20	21	22	23	24
	25	26	27	28	29	30	31

Cream of Broccoli Soup

Makes 2 servings, about 1 cup each

2 cups sliced trimmed broccoli (stems and florets)
Water
2 teaspoons margarine
1 tablespoon *each* minced shallot *or* onion and all-purpose flour

1½ cups low-fat milk (1% milk fat)
1 tablespoon dry sherry
¼ teaspoon salt
Dash *each* white pepper and ground nutmeg

Microwave Method: In 1½-quart microwavable casserole combine broccoli and ¼ cup water. Cover with vented plastic wrap and microwave on High (100%) for 7 minutes until broccoli is tender; set aside.

In medium microwavable mixing bowl combine margarine and shallot (or onion) and microwave on High for 40 seconds; add flour and, using a wire whisk, stir until mixture is smooth and thoroughly combined. Stir in milk. Cover with vented plastic wrap and microwave on High for 4 minutes, stirring thoroughly every minute. Transfer milk mixture to work bowl of food processor; add broccoli mixture and process until mixture is pureed. Pour soup back into bowl; stir in sherry and seasonings and microwave on High for 1 minute until heated through.

Conventional Method: Set steamer insert in 2-quart saucepan; add 1½ cups water (water should not touch insert). Arrange broccoli in insert, cover, and bring to a boil. Cook until broccoli is tender, about 5 minutes.

While broccoli is steaming, in 2-quart saucepan melt margarine; add shallot (or onion) and sauté over medium-high heat until translucent, about 45 seconds. Add flour and stir quickly to combine. Using a wire whisk, gradually stir in milk; cook over medium-high heat, stirring constantly, until mixture thickens slightly, about 5 minutes. Transfer to work bowl of food processor; add broccoli and process until pureed. Pour soup back into saucepan; stir in sherry and seasonings and cook over medium heat until heated through, about 1 minute.

Each serving provides: 2 Vegetable Exchanges; 1 Fat Exchange; ¾ Milk Exchange; 40 Optional Calories
Per serving: 165 calories; 9 g protein; 6 g fat; 18 g carbohydrate; 274 mg calcium; 431 mg sodium; 7 mg cholesterol; 1 g dietary fiber

Caribbean Plantain and Beef Casserole

Makes 2 servings

- ¼ cup *each* chopped onion and green bell pepper
- 1 teaspoon olive *or* vegetable oil
- 1 garlic clove, minced
- 3 ounces cooked ground beef, crumbled
- 1 ounce diced cooked ham
- ¼ cup tomato sauce
- 3 pimiento-stuffed green olives, chopped
- 1 tablespoon drained capers, rinsed
- 1 egg, beaten with 1 tablespoon water
- ½ teaspoon oregano leaves
- 3 ounces peeled plantain, cut lengthwise into 6 slices

Microwave Method: In 2-quart microwavable casserole combine onion, bell pepper, oil, and garlic; stir well to thoroughly combine. Microwave on High (100%) for 1 minute. Stir in beef, ham, tomato sauce, olives, and capers; microwave on High for 2 minutes until flavors blend. Let cool slightly; stir in egg mixture and oregano.

Spray 7-inch microwavable pie plate with nonstick cooking spray. Spread meat mixture in plate; top with plantain. Cover with vented plastic wrap; microwave on Medium (50%) for 8 minutes, rotating plate ½ turn halfway through cooking. Let stand covered for 3 minutes.

Conventional Method: Preheat oven to 350°F. In 9-inch nonstick skillet heat oil over high heat; add onion, bell pepper, garlic, and ham and sauté until vegetables are softened, 1 to 2 minutes. Stir in beef, tomato sauce, olives, capers, and oregano and cook, stirring occasionally, until mixture is heated through, 2 to 3 minutes. Let cool slightly; stir in egg mixture.

Spray shallow 1-quart casserole with nonstick cooking spray. Spread meat mixture in casserole; top with plantain. Bake until heated through and lightly browned, 40 to 45 minutes.

Each serving provides: 2½ Protein Exchanges; ½ Bread Exchange; ¾ Vegetable Exchange; ½ Fat Exchange; 10 Optional Calories

Per serving: 282 calories; 17 g protein; 16 g fat; 19 g carbohydrate; 42 mg calcium; 636 mg sodium; 182 mg cholesterol; 1 g dietary fiber

WEIGHT
RECIPE
WATCHERS

Raspberry Pudding Pie

Makes 8 servings

2 tablespoons plus 2 teaspoons
 margarine
16 graham crackers (2½-inch squares),
 made into fine crumbs
¼ cup reduced-calorie raspberry
 spread (16 calories per 2 teaspoons)

1 cup skim *or* nonfat milk
½ cup plain low-fat yogurt
1 envelope (four ½-cup servings)
 reduced-calorie vanilla instant
 pudding mix

Microwave Method: Spray 9-inch microwavable pie plate with nonstick cooking spray; set aside. In small microwavable bowl microwave margarine on High (100%) for 30 seconds until melted; stir in crumbs until moistened. Using the back of a spoon, press crumb mixture over bottom and up sides of sprayed pie plate; microwave on High for 1 minute. Cover center of crust with sheet of aluminum foil; rotate pie plate ½ turn and microwave on High 1 minute longer. Set aside and let cool.

In small microwavable bowl microwave raspberry spread on High for 1 minute, stirring after 30 seconds; set aside. In blender container combine remaining ingredients and process until combined; pour into cooled crust. Spread raspberry spread over pudding; cover and refrigerate until firm, about 1 hour.

Conventional Method: Preheat oven to 350°F. Spray 9-inch glass pie plate with nonstick cooking spray; set aside.

In small saucepan melt margarine; remove from heat and stir in crumbs until moistened. Using the back of a spoon, press crumb mixture over bottom and up sides of sprayed pie plate. Bake until crust is crisp and brown, 4 to 5 minutes; set aside and let cool.

In small saucepan cook raspberry spread over low heat, stirring constantly, until melted; set aside. In blender container combine remaining ingredients and process until combined; pour into cooled crust. Spread raspberry spread over pudding; cover and refrigerate until firm, about 1 hour.

Each serving provides: 1 Bread Exchange; 1 Fat Exchange; ½ Milk Exchange; 10 Optional Calories

Per serving: 133 calories; 3 g protein; 5 g fat; 19 g carbohydrate; 71 mg calcium; 331 mg sodium; 1 mg cholesterol; 1 g dietary fiber

Dutch Mint Coffee

Makes 2 servings, about 1 cup each

1 envelope (1 serving) reduced-calorie chocolate marshmallow-flavored hot cocoa mix
1 cup skim *or* nonfat milk
2 tablespoons white mint-flavored liqueur

1 cup strong coffee (*hot*)
2 tablespoons thawed frozen dairy whipped topping
⅛ ounce (about 1 tablespoon) chocolate, grated

Microwave Method: Using a wire whisk, in medium microwavable bowl combine cocoa mix, milk, and liqueur, stirring to dissolve cocoa. Microwave on High (100%) for 2 minutes until hot but not boiling; stir in coffee. Divide into two 10-ounce mugs. Spoon half of the whipped topping onto each serving of coffee. Sprinkle each serving with half of the chocolate and serve immediately.

Conventional Method: Using a wire whisk, in 1-quart saucepan combine cocoa mix, milk, and liqueur and cook over high heat, stirring occasionally, until mixture is hot but not boiling, 2 to 3 minutes; stir in coffee. Divide into two 10-ounce mugs. Spoon half of the whipped topping onto each serving of coffee. Sprinkle each serving with half of the chocolate and serve immediately.

Each serving provides: 1 Milk Exchange; 70 Optional Calories

Per serving: 159 calories; 7 g protein; 2 g fat; 20 g carbohydrate; 307 mg calcium; 154 mg sodium; 3 mg cholesterol; 0 g dietary fiber

MARCH

SUNDAY	MONDAY	TUESDAY	WEDNESDAY
4	5	6	7
11	12	13	14
18	19	20	21
25	26	27	28

MARCH

THURSDAY	FRIDAY	SATURDAY
1	2	3
8	9	10
15	16	17
22	23	24
29	30	31

*Microwave
Menu
of the Month*

Baked Pork
Chop
with
Applesauce

Cooked Cabbage
Wedge and
Carrot Chunks
sprinkled with
Caraway Seed

Cucumber Slices on Bibb
Lettuce with Reduced-
Calorie Butermilk
Dressing

Irish Bread Pudding

Light Beer

NOTES/GOALS

WEEKLY FOOD DIARY

	MONDAY	TUESDAY	WEDNESDAY	THURSDAY	FRIDAY	SATURDAY	SUNDAY
DAILY TOTALS	FRUIT ___ VEG ___ FAT ___ PROTEIN ___ BREAD ___ MILK ___ FLOATING ___	FRUIT ___ VEG ___ FAT ___ PROTEIN ___ BREAD ___ MILK ___ FLOATING ___	FRUIT ___ VEG ___ FAT ___ PROTEIN ___ BREAD ___ MILK ___ FLOATING ___	FRUIT ___ VEG ___ FAT ___ PROTEIN ___ BREAD ___ MILK ___ FLOATING ___	FRUIT ___ VEG ___ FAT ___ PROTEIN ___ BREAD ___ MILK ___ FLOATING ___	FRUIT ___ VEG ___ FAT ___ PROTEIN ___ BREAD ___ MILK ___ FLOATING ___	FRUIT ___ VEG ___ FAT ___ PROTEIN ___ BREAD ___ MILK ___ FLOATING ___
BREAKFAST							
LUNCH							
DINNER							
SNACKS							

WEEKLY LIMITS EGGS _____ CHEESE _____ MEAT _____ ORGAN MEAT _____ OPTIONAL CALORIES _____

I will attend my Weight Watchers meeting this week on _____

MONDAY
26

TUESDAY
27

Ash Wednesday

WEDNESDAY
28

THURSDAY
1

FRIDAY
2

SATURDAY
3

SUNDAY
4

	S	M	T	W	T	F	S
					1	2	3
F	4	5	6	7	8	9	10
E	11	12	13	14	15	16	17
B	18	19	20	21	22	23	24
	25	26	27	28			

	S	M	T	W	T	F	S
					1	2	3
M	4	5	6	7	8	9	10
A	11	12	13	14	15	16	17
R	18	19	20	21	22	23	24
	25	26	27	28	29	30	31

	S	M	T	W	T	F	S
	1	2	3	4	5	6	7
A	8	9	10	11	12	13	14
P	15	16	17	18	19	20	21
R	22	23	24	25	26	27	28
	29	30					

WEEKLY FOOD DIARY

	MONDAY	TUESDAY	WEDNESDAY	THURSDAY	FRIDAY	SATURDAY	SUNDAY
DAILY TOTALS	FRUIT ___ VEG ___ FAT ___ PROTEIN ___ BREAD ___ MILK ___ FLOATING ___	FRUIT ___ VEG ___ FAT ___ PROTEIN ___ BREAD ___ MILK ___ FLOATING ___	FRUIT ___ VEG ___ FAT ___ PROTEIN ___ BREAD ___ MILK ___ FLOATING ___	FRUIT ___ VEG ___ FAT ___ PROTEIN ___ BREAD ___ MILK ___ FLOATING ___	FRUIT ___ VEG ___ FAT ___ PROTEIN ___ BREAD ___ MILK ___ FLOATING ___	FRUIT ___ VEG ___ FAT ___ PROTEIN ___ BREAD ___ MILK ___ FLOATING ___	FRUIT ___ VEG ___ FAT ___ PROTEIN ___ BREAD ___ MILK ___ FLOATING ___
BREAKFAST							
LUNCH							
DINNER							
SNACKS							

WEEKLY LIMITS   EGGS _____   CHEESE _____   MEAT _____   ORGAN MEAT _____   OPTIONAL CALORIES _____

I will attend my Weight Watchers meeting this week on _____

ENGAGEMENTS

MARCH

1990

MONDAY
5

TUESDAY
6

WEDNESDAY
7

THURSDAY
8

FRIDAY
9

SATURDAY
10

SUNDAY
11

	S	M	T	W	T	F	S
					1	2	3
F	4	5	6	7	8	9	10
E	11	12	13	14	15	16	17
B	18	19	20	21	22	23	24
	25	26	27	28			

	S	M	T	W	T	F	S
					1	2	3
M	4	5	6	7	8	9	10
A	11	12	13	14	15	16	17
R	18	19	20	21	22	23	24
	25	26	27	28	29	30	31

	S	M	T	W	T	F	S
A	1	2	3	4	5	6	7
P	8	9	10	11	12	13	14
R	15	16	17	18	19	20	21
	22	23	24	25	26	27	28
	29	30					

WEEKLY FOOD DIARY

	MONDAY	TUESDAY	WEDNESDAY	THURSDAY	FRIDAY	SATURDAY	SUNDAY
DAILY TOTALS			FRUIT ____ VEG ____ FAT ____ PROTEIN ____ BREAD ____ MILK ____ FLOATING ____	FRUIT ____ VEG ____ FAT ____ PROTEIN ____ BREAD ____ MILK ____ FLOATING ____	FRUIT ____ VEG ____ FAT ____ PROTEIN ____ BREAD ____ MILK ____ FLOATING ____	FRUIT ____ VEG ____ FAT ____ PROTEIN ____ BREAD ____ MILK ____ FLOATING ____	FRUIT ____ VEG ____ FAT ____ PROTEIN ____ BREAD ____ MILK ____ FLOATING ____
BREAKFAST							
LUNCH							
DINNER							
SNACKS							

WEEKLY LIMITS   EGGS ____   CHEESE ____   MEAT ____   ORGAN MEAT ____   OPTIONAL CALORIES ____

I will attend my Weight Watchers meeting this week on ____

E N G A G E M E N T S

MARCH

1 9 9 0

MONDAY
12

TUESDAY
13

WEDNESDAY
14

THURSDAY
15

FRIDAY
16

St. Patrick's Day

SATURDAY
17

SUNDAY
18

	S	M	T	W	T	F	S
					1	2	3
F	4	5	6	7	8	9	10
E	11	12	13	14	15	16	17
B	18	19	20	21	22	23	24
	25	26	27	28			

	S	M	T	W	T	F	S
					1	2	3
M	4	5	6	7	8	9	10
A	11	12	13	14	15	16	17
R	18	19	20	21	22	23	24
	25	26	27	28	29	30	31

	S	M	T	W	T	F	S
	1	2	3	4	5	6	7
A	8	9	10	11	12	13	14
P	15	16	17	18	19	20	21
R	22	23	24	25	26	27	28
	29	30					

WEEKLY FOOD DIARY

	MONDAY	TUESDAY	WEDNESDAY	THURSDAY	FRIDAY	SATURDAY	SUNDAY
DAILY TOTALS			FRUIT ____ VEG ____ FAT ____ PROTEIN ____ BREAD ____ MILK ____ FLOATING ____	FRUIT ____ VEG ____ FAT ____ PROTEIN ____ BREAD ____ MILK ____ FLOATING ____	FRUIT ____ VEG ____ FAT ____ PROTEIN ____ BREAD ____ MILK ____ FLOATING ____	FRUIT ____ VEG ____ FAT ____ PROTEIN ____ BREAD ____ MILK ____ FLOATING ____	FRUIT ____ VEG ____ FAT ____ PROTEIN ____ BREAD ____ MILK ____ FLOATING ____
BREAKFAST				Cereal Bread			
LUNCH				Salad Ry-Krisp (1)			
DINNER				Salad Ry-Krisp (1)			
SNACKS							

WEEKLY LIMITS EGGS ____   CHEESE ____   MEAT ____   ORGAN MEAT ____   OPTIONAL CALORIES ____

I will attend my **Weight Watchers** meeting this week on ____

ENGAGEMENTS

MARCH

1 9 9 0

MONDAY
19

TUESDAY
20

WEDNESDAY
21

THURSDAY
22

FRIDAY
23

SATURDAY
24

SUNDAY
25

	S	M	T	W	T	F	S
					1	2	3
F	4	5	6	7	8	9	10
E	11	12	13	14	15	16	17
B	18	19	20	21	22	23	24
	25	26	27	28			

	S	M	T	W	T	F	S
					1	2	3
M	4	5	6	7	8	9	10
A	11	12	13	14	15	16	17
R	18	19	20	21	22	23	24
	25	26	27	28	29	30	31

	S	M	T	W	T	F	S
	1	2	3	4	5	6	7
A	8	9	10	11	12	13	14
P	15	16	17	18	19	20	21
R	22	23	24	25	26	27	28
	29	30					

WEEKLY FOOD DIARY

	MONDAY	TUESDAY	WEDNESDAY	THURSDAY	FRIDAY	SATURDAY	SUNDAY
DAILY TOTALS	FRUIT ___ VEG ___ FAT ___ PROTEIN ___ BREAD ___ MILK ___ FLOATING ___	FRUIT ___ VEG ___ FAT ___ PROTEIN ___ BREAD ___ MILK ___ FLOATING ___	FRUIT ___ VEG ___ FAT ___ PROTEIN ___ BREAD ___ MILK ___ FLOATING ___	FRUIT ___ VEG ___ FAT ___ PROTEIN ___ BREAD ___ MILK ___ FLOATING ___	FRUIT ___ VEG ___ FAT ___ PROTEIN ___ BREAD ___ MILK ___ FLOATING ___	FRUIT ___ VEG ___ FAT ___ PROTEIN ___ BREAD ___ MILK ___ FLOATING ___	FRUIT ___ VEG ___ FAT ___ PROTEIN ___ BREAD ___ MILK ___ FLOATING ___
BREAKFAST							
LUNCH							
DINNER							
SNACKS							

WEEKLY LIMITS EGGS ___ CHEESE ___ MEAT ___ ORGAN MEAT ___ OPTIONAL CALORIES ___

I will attend my Weight Watchers meeting this week on ___

ENGAGEMENTS

MARCH
APRIL

1 9 9 0

MONDAY
26

TUESDAY
27

WEDNESDAY
28

THURSDAY
29

FRIDAY
30

SATURDAY
31

SUNDAY
1

	S	M	T	W	T	F	S
					1	2	3
F	4	5	6	7	8	9	10
E	11	12	13	14	15	16	17
B	18	19	20	21	22	23	24
	25	26	27	28			

	S	M	T	W	T	F	S
					1	2	3
M	4	5	6	7	8	9	10
A	11	12	13	14	15	16	17
R	18	19	20	21	22	23	24
	25	26	27	28	29	30	31

	S	M	T	W	T	F	S
	1	2	3	4	5	6	7
A	8	9	10	11	12	13	14
P	15	16	17	18	19	20	21
R	22	23	24	25	26	27	28
	29	30					

WEIGHT
·RECIPE·
WATCHERS

Asparagus Polonaise

Makes 2 servings

- **18 asparagus spears (woody ends removed)**
- **1 tablespoon freshly squeezed lemon juice**
- **½ teaspoon salt**
- **1 tablespoon whipped butter**
- **3 tablespoons seasoned dried bread crumbs**
- **1 hard-cooked egg, chopped**
- **1 tablespoon chopped Italian (flat-leaf) parsley**

Microwave Method: In 13 × 9 × 2-inch microwavable baking dish arrange asparagus in a single layer with tips in center of dish; cover with vented plastic wrap and microwave on High (100%) for 4 minutes, rotating dish ½ turn halfway through cooking. Carefully remove plastic wrap; sprinkle asparagus with lemon juice and salt. Re-cover and let stand for 2 minutes.

In small microwavable mixing bowl microwave butter on High for 30 seconds until melted; add bread crumbs and stir to moisten. Add egg and parsley and stir to combine. Sprinkle over asparagus.

Conventional Method: In 10-inch skillet bring 2 cups water to a boil; add asparagus, lemon juice, and salt and cook over medium heat until tender, 10 to 15 minutes.

In small saucepan melt butter; add bread crumbs and cook over medium heat, stirring constantly, until bread crumbs are golden brown, about 2 minutes. Remove from heat; add egg and parsley and stir to combine.

To serve, drain asparagus and arrange on serving platter; sprinkle with egg mixture.

Each serving provides: ½ Protein Exchange; ½ Bread Exchange; 1½ Vegetable Exchanges; 25 Optional Calories

Per serving: 141 calories; 8 g protein; 6 g fat; 15 g carbohydrate; 64 mg calcium; 915 mg sodium; 145 mg cholesterol; 5 g dietary fiber

Scrod Areganata

Makes 2 servings

2 scrod fillets (¼ pound each)
3 tablespoons plain dried bread crumbs
1 tablespoon *each* grated Parmesan
   cheese and chopped fresh parsley
½ teaspoon oregano leaves
⅛ teaspoon *each* salt and pepper

¼ cup dry white table wine
2 teaspoons olive *or* vegetable oil
1 teaspoon freshly squeezed lemon
   juice
1 garlic clove, minced

Microwave Method: In 1-quart microwavable casserole arrange fish. In small mixing bowl combine bread crumbs, cheese, parsley, oregano, salt, and pepper and sprinkle over fish; set aside. In 1-cup microwavable liquid measuring cup combine wine, oil, lemon juice, and garlic and microwave on High (100%) for 45 seconds. Pour wine mixture evenly over bread crumb mixture; cover with vented plastic wrap and microwave on High for 4 minutes, rotating casserole ½ turn halfway through cooking. Let stand for 1½ minutes, until fish is opaque and flakes easily when tested with a fork.

Conventional Method: Preheat oven to 400°F. Spray 1-quart casserole with nonstick cooking spray; arrange fish in casserole. In small mixing bowl combine bread crumbs, cheese, parsley, oregano, salt, and pepper and sprinkle over fish; set aside.

In small saucepan heat oil; add garlic and sauté over medium heat until softened, about 1 minute. Add wine and lemon juice; pour wine mixture evenly over bread crumb mixture. Bake for 15 minutes, until fish is opaque and flakes easily when tested with a fork.

Each serving provides: 3 Protein Exchanges; ½ Bread Exchange; 1 Fat Exchange; 45 Optional Calories
Per serving: 206 calories; 23 g protein; 6 g fat; 8 g carbohydrate; 79 mg calcium; 318 mg sodium; 51 mg cholesterol; 0.1 g dietary fiber

Minted Lamb Stew

Makes 2 servings

4½ ounces diced pared red potatoes
½ cup *each* sliced carrot (½-inch pieces) and cubed turnip
¼ cup sliced thoroughly washed leek (white portion only)
1 teaspoon olive *or* vegetable oil
1 garlic clove, minced
½ cup canned ready-to-serve chicken broth

¼ cup water
1 tablespoon *each* all-purpose flour and chopped fresh mint *or* 1 teaspoon mint flakes
6 ounces cooked cubed lamb
¼ cup frozen tiny peas
Dash white pepper

Microwave Method: In 3-quart microwavable casserole combine potatoes, carrot, turnip, leek, oil, and garlic; stir well to thoroughly combine. Cover with vented plastic wrap and microwave on High (100%) for 2 minutes. In 1-cup liquid measure combine broth, water, flour, and mint, stirring to dissolve flour; pour into casserole. Replace vented plastic wrap and microwave on High for 5 minutes, stirring mixture and rotating casserole ½ turn after 2 minutes. Add lamb and peas and stir to combine; re-cover with vented plastic wrap. Microwave on Medium (50%) for 4 minutes until lamb and peas are heated through and vegetables are tender. Stir in pepper.

Conventional Method: In 3-quart saucepan heat oil over medium-high heat; add potatoes, carrot, turnip, leek, and garlic and sauté until vegetables are tender-crisp, 1 to 2 minutes. Sprinkle flour over vegetables and stir quickly to combine; stir in broth and water and cook, stirring frequently, until flour is dissolved. Add lamb and stir to combine. Reduce heat to low, cover, and let simmer, stirring occasionally, until mixture thickens, about 15 minutes. Add mint, peas, and pepper and cook until peas are heated through, 2 to 3 minutes.

Each serving provides: 3 Protein Exchanges; 1 Bread Exchange; 1¼ Vegetable Exchanges; ½ Fat Exchange; 25 Optional Calories

Per serving: 304 calories; 28 g protein; 10 g fat; 26 g carbohydrate; 46 mg calcium; 384 mg sodium; 85 mg cholesterol; 4 g dietary fiber

Irish Bread Pudding

Makes 2 servings

4 slices reduced-calorie *or* light
  cinnamon raisin bread (40 calories
  per slice), cubed
½ cup *each* evaporated skimmed milk
  and low-fat milk (1% milk fat)
1 egg

3 tablespoons Irish whiskey
2 tablespoons plus 2 teaspoons instant
  nonfat dry milk powder
1 teaspoon granulated sugar
½ teaspoon caraway seed

Microwave Method: Spray two 10-ounce microwavable custard cups with nonstick cooking spray. Arrange half of the bread cubes in each cup; set aside.

Using a wire whisk, in medium mixing bowl combine remaining ingredients, beating well. Pour half of mixture into each prepared cup. Set cups in 8 × 8 × 2-inch microwavable baking dish and pour water into dish to a depth of about 1 inch; microwave on Medium (50%) for 17 minutes (until a knife, inserted in center, comes out clean). Let stand for 1 minute. Remove cups from water bath and let pudding stand at room temperature for 5 minutes. Cover with plastic wrap and refrigerate until chilled, at least 30 minutes.

Conventional Method: Preheat oven to 350°F. Spray two 10-ounce custard cups with nonstick cooking spray. Arrange half of the bread cubes in each cup; set aside.

Using a wire whisk, in medium mixing bowl combine remaining ingredients, beating well. Pour half of mixture into each prepared cup. Set cups in 8 × 8 × 2-inch baking pan and pour water into pan to a depth of about 1 inch; bake for 40 to 45 minutes (until a knife, inserted in center, comes out clean). Remove baking pan from oven and cups from water bath; let pudding stand at room temperature for 5 minutes. Cover with plastic wrap and refrigerate until chilled, at least 30 minutes.

Each serving provides: ½ Protein Exchange; 1 Bread Exchange; 1 Milk Exchange; 75 Optional Calories
Per serving: 277 calories; 16 g protein; 4 g fat; 34 g carbohydrate; 388 mg calcium; 360 mg sodium; 143 mg cholesterol; 0 g dietary fiber

APRIL

SUNDAY	MONDAY	TUESDAY	WEDNESDAY
1	2	3	4
8	9	10	11
15	16	17	18
22	23	24	25
29	30		

THURSDAY	FRIDAY	SATURDAY
5	6	7
12	13	14
19	20	21
26	27	28

Microwave Menu of the Month

Gefilte Fish Balls with Horseradish on Shredded Lettuce

Matzo Torte

Cooked Asparagus Spears sprinkled with Sesame Seed

Fresh Fruit Salad

Tea with Honey

NOTES/GOALS

WEEKLY FOOD DIARY

	MONDAY	TUESDAY	WEDNESDAY	THURSDAY	FRIDAY	SATURDAY	SUNDAY
DAILY TOTALS	FRUIT ___ VEG ___ FAT ___ PROTEIN ___ BREAD ___ MILK ___ FLOATING ___	FRUIT ___ VEG ___ FAT ___ PROTEIN ___ BREAD ___ MILK ___ FLOATING ___	FRUIT ___ VEG ___ FAT ___ PROTEIN ___ BREAD ___ MILK ___ FLOATING ___	FRUIT ___ VEG ___ FAT ___ PROTEIN ___ BREAD ___ MILK ___ FLOATING ___	FRUIT ___ VEG ___ FAT ___ PROTEIN ___ BREAD ___ MILK ___ FLOATING ___	FRUIT ___ VEG ___ FAT ___ PROTEIN ___ BREAD ___ MILK ___ FLOATING ___	FRUIT ___ VEG ___ FAT ___ PROTEIN ___ BREAD ___ MILK ___ FLOATING ___
BREAKFAST							
LUNCH							
DINNER							
SNACKS							

WEEKLY LIMITS   EGGS ___   CHEESE ___   MEAT ___   ORGAN MEAT ___   OPTIONAL CALORIES ___

I will attend my Weight Watchers meeting this week on _____

ENGAGEMENTS

APRIL

1 9 9 0

MONDAY
2

TUESDAY
3

WEDNESDAY
4

THURSDAY
5

FRIDAY
6

SATURDAY
7

Palm Sunday

SUNDAY
8

	S	M	T	W	T	F	S
						1	2	3
M	4	5	6	7	8	9	10
A	11	12	13	14	15	16	17
R	18	19	20	21	22	23	24
	25	26	27	28	29	30	31

	S	M	T	W	T	F	S
	1	2	3	4	5	6	7
A	8	9	10	11	12	13	14
P	15	16	17	18	19	20	21
R	22	23	24	25	26	27	28
	29	30					

	S	M	T	W	T	F	S
			1	2	3	4	5
M	6	7	8	9	10	11	12
A	13	14	15	16	17	18	19
Y	20	21	22	23	24	25	26
	27	28	29	30	31		

WEEKLY FOOD DIARY

	MONDAY	TUESDAY	WEDNESDAY	THURSDAY	FRIDAY	SATURDAY	SUNDAY
DAILY TOTALS	FRUIT ___ VEG ___ FAT ___ PROTEIN ___ BREAD ___ MILK ___ FLOATING ___	FRUIT ___ VEG ___ FAT ___ PROTEIN ___ BREAD ___ MILK ___ FLOATING ___	FRUIT ___ VEG ___ FAT ___ PROTEIN ___ BREAD ___ MILK ___ FLOATING ___	FRUIT ___ VEG ___ FAT ___ PROTEIN ___ BREAD ___ MILK ___ FLOATING ___	FRUIT ___ VEG ___ FAT ___ PROTEIN ___ BREAD ___ MILK ___ FLOATING ___	FRUIT ___ VEG ___ FAT ___ PROTEIN ___ BREAD ___ MILK ___ FLOATING ___	FRUIT ___ VEG ___ FAT ___ PROTEIN ___ BREAD ___ MILK ___ FLOATING ___
BREAKFAST							
LUNCH							
DINNER							
SNACKS							

WEEKLY LIMITS EGGS _____ CHEESE _____ MEAT _____ ORGAN MEAT _____ OPTIONAL CALORIES _____

I will attend my Weight Watchers meeting this week on _____

MONDAY
9

First Day of Passover

TUESDAY
10

WEDNESDAY
11

THURSDAY
12

Good Friday

FRIDAY
13

SATURDAY
14

Easter Sunday

SUNDAY
15

	S	M	T	W	T	F	S
						1	2	3
M	4	5	6	7	8	9	10
A	11	12	13	14	15	16	17
R	18	19	20	21	22	23	24
	25	26	27	28	29	30	31

	S	M	T	W	T	F	S
	1	2	3	4	5	6	7
A	8	9	10	11	12	13	14
P	15	16	17	18	19	20	21
R	22	23	24	25	26	27	28
	29	30					

	S	M	T	W	T	F	S
			1	2	3	4	5
M	6	7	8	9	10	11	12
A	13	14	15	16	17	18	19
Y	20	21	22	23	24	25	26
	27	28	29	30	31		

WEEKLY FOOD DIARY

	MONDAY	TUESDAY	WEDNESDAY	THURSDAY	FRIDAY	SATURDAY	SUNDAY
DAILY TOTALS	FRUIT ___ VEG ___ FAT ___ PROTEIN ___ BREAD ___ MILK ___ FLOATING ___	FRUIT ___ VEG ___ FAT ___ PROTEIN ___ BREAD ___ MILK ___ FLOATING ___	FRUIT ___ VEG ___ FAT ___ PROTEIN ___ BREAD ___ MILK ___ FLOATING ___	FRUIT ___ VEG ___ FAT ___ PROTEIN ___ BREAD ___ MILK ___ FLOATING ___	FRUIT ___ VEG ___ FAT ___ PROTEIN ___ BREAD ___ MILK ___ FLOATING ___	FRUIT ___ VEG ___ FAT ___ PROTEIN ___ BREAD ___ MILK ___ FLOATING ___	FRUIT ___ VEG ___ FAT ___ PROTEIN ___ BREAD ___ MILK ___ FLOATING ___
BREAKFAST							
LUNCH							
DINNER							
SNACKS							

WEEKLY LIMITS   EGGS ___   CHEESE ___   MEAT ___   ORGAN MEAT ___   OPTIONAL CALORIES ___

I will attend my Weight Watchers meeting this week on ___

APRIL

1 9 9 0

Easter Monday (Canada)

MONDAY
16

TUESDAY
17

WEDNESDAY
18

THURSDAY
19

FRIDAY
20

SATURDAY
21

SUNDAY
22

	S	M	T	W	T	F	S
M						1	2	3
A	4	5	6	7	8	9	10
R	11	12	13	14	15	16	17
	18	19	20	21	22	23	24
	25	26	27	28	29	30	31

	S	M	T	W	T	F	S
		1	2	3	4	5	6	7
A	8	9	10	11	12	13	14
P	15	16	17	18	19	20	21
R	22	23	24	25	26	27	28
	29	30					

	S	M	T	W	T	F	S
M			1	2	3	4	5
A	6	7	8	9	10	11	12
Y	13	14	15	16	17	18	19
	20	21	22	23	24	25	26
	27	28	29	30	31		

WEEKLY FOOD DIARY

	MONDAY	TUESDAY	WEDNESDAY	THURSDAY	FRIDAY	SATURDAY	SUNDAY
DAILY TOTALS	FRUIT ——— VEG ——— FAT ——— PROTEIN ——— BREAD ——— MILK ——— FLOATING ———	FRUIT ——— VEG ——— FAT ——— PROTEIN ——— BREAD ——— MILK ——— FLOATING ———	FRUIT ——— VEG ——— FAT ——— PROTEIN ——— BREAD ——— MILK ——— FLOATING ———	FRUIT ——— VEG ——— FAT ——— PROTEIN ——— BREAD ——— MILK ——— FLOATING ———	FRUIT ——— VEG ——— FAT ——— PROTEIN ——— BREAD ——— MILK ——— FLOATING ———	FRUIT ——— VEG ——— FAT ——— PROTEIN ——— BREAD ——— MILK ——— FLOATING ———	FRUIT ——— VEG ——— FAT ——— PROTEIN ——— BREAD ——— MILK ——— FLOATING ———
BREAKFAST							
LUNCH							
DINNER							
SNACKS							

WEEKLY LIMITS   EGGS ———   CHEESE ———   MEAT ———   ORGAN MEAT ———   OPTIONAL CALORIES ———

I will attend my Weight Watchers meeting this week on ————————

APRIL

1 9 9 0

MONDAY
23

TUESDAY
24

WEDNESDAY
25

THURSDAY
26

FRIDAY
27

SATURDAY
28

SUNDAY
29

	S	M	T	W	T	F	S
						1	2	3
M	4	5	6	7	8	9	10
A	11	12	13	14	15	16	17
R	18	19	20	21	22	23	24
	25	26	27	28	29	30	31

	S	M	T	W	T	F	S
	1	2	3	4	5	6	7
A	8	9	10	11	12	13	14
P	15	16	17	18	19	20	21
R	22	23	24	25	26	27	28
	29	30					

	S	M	T	W	T	F	S
			1	2	3	4	5
M	6	7	8	9	10	11	12
A	13	14	15	16	17	18	19
Y	20	21	22	23	24	25	26
	27	28	29	30	31		

WEIGHT
RECIPE
WATCHERS

Bacon-Cheese Appetizers

Makes 2 servings, 6 appetizers each

1 ounce Swiss cheese, shredded
2 slices crisp bacon, crumbled
4 pimiento-stuffed green olives, minced
2 teaspoons minced red onion

½ teaspoon seeded and minced chili pepper *or* **⅛ teaspoon crushed red pepper**
12 melba rounds

Microwave Method: In small mixing bowl combine all ingredients except melba rounds. Onto each melba round spoon an equal amount of cheese mixture. Arrange melba rounds in a circle on microwavable plate and microwave on High (100%) for 30 to 45 seconds until cheese begins to melt, rotating plate ½ turn after 20 seconds.

Conventional Method: In small mixing bowl combine all ingredients except melba rounds. Onto each melba round spoon an equal amount of cheese mixture. Arrange melba rounds on nonstick baking sheet and broil until cheese is melted, about 30 seconds.

Each serving provides: ½ Protein Exchange; 1 Bread Exchange; 55 Optional Calories

Per serving: 171 calories; 9 g protein; 9 g fat; 14 g carbohydrate; 145 mg calcium; 282 mg sodium; 18 mg cholesterol; 0.2 g dietary fiber (this figure does not include melba rounds; nutrition analysis not available)

Artichoke Soup

Makes 2 servings, about ¾ cup each

2 cups (9-ounce package) frozen artichoke hearts (remove and discard tough outer leaves)
Water
1 cup canned ready-to-serve chicken broth
4 ounces drained canned white beans

1 garlic clove, chopped
2 tablespoons half-and-half (blend of milk and cream)
1 tablespoon minced fresh basil *or* **½ teaspoon basil leaves**
1 teaspoon freshly squeezed lemon juice

Microwave Method: In 1-quart microwavable casserole combine artichoke hearts and 2 tablespoons water; cover with vented plastic wrap and microwave on High (100%) for 7 minutes until artichokes are tender, stirring once halfway through cooking. Transfer artichokes and cooking liquid to work bowl of food processor; add broth, beans, and garlic and process until pureed, scraping down sides of container as necessary, about 1½ minutes. Return to casserole and stir in remaining ingredients. Cover casserole with vented plastic wrap and microwave on High for 3 minutes, stirring halfway through cooking, until mixture is heated through.

Conventional Method: In 2-quart saucepan combine artichokes and ¼ cup water and bring to a boil. Reduce heat to medium and let simmer until tender, 8 to 10 minutes. Transfer artichokes and cooking liquid to work bowl of food processor; add broth, beans, and garlic and process until pureed, scraping down sides of container as necessary, about 1½ minutes. Return to saucepan and stir in remaining ingredients. Cook over medium-high heat, stirring occasionally, until mixture is heated through, about 5 minutes.

Each serving provides: 1 Protein Exchange; 2 Vegetable Exchanges; 45 Optional Calories

Per serving: 155 calories; 9 g protein; 4 g fat; 25 g carbohydrate; 92 mg calcium; 571 mg sodium; 6 mg cholesterol; 5 g dietary fiber (this figure does not include white beans; nutrition analysis not available)

WEIGHT
RECIPE
WATCHERS

Salad of Salmon and Asparagus

Makes 2 servings

6 asparagus spears (woody ends removed), cut into 2-inch pieces
¼ cup water
2 tablespoons freshly squeezed lemon juice
½ pound skinned salmon fillet (about 1 inch thick)
2 tablespoons *each* skim *or* nonfat milk and sour cream

1 tablespoon plus 1 teaspoon reduced-calorie mayonnaise
1 tablespoon prepared horseradish
1 teaspoon drained capers
2 cups torn lettuce leaves
¼ cup sliced red onion

Microwave Method: In 8 × 8 × 2-inch microwavable baking dish arrange asparagus; sprinkle with water and lemon juice. Cover with vented plastic wrap and microwave on High (100%) for 1 minute until tender-crisp. Arrange salmon in dish over asparagus, replace vented plastic wrap, and microwave on High for 3 minutes, until fish flakes easily when tested with a fork. Remove from oven and let stand for 1 minute. Using a slotted spoon, transfer salmon and asparagus to plate; cover and refrigerate until chilled, at least 30 minutes.

In small mixing bowl combine milk, sour cream, mayonnaise, horseradish, and capers; mix well. Line serving platter with lettuce; decoratively arrange salmon, asparagus, and onion on platter. Top with dressing.

Conventional Method: In 8-inch nonstick skillet combine water and lemon juice and bring to a boil; add salmon, reduce heat to low, and let simmer for 3 to 4 minutes. Arrange asparagus around salmon in skillet and continue to simmer, until fish flakes easily when tested with a fork and asparagus are tender-crisp, 3 to 4 minutes longer. Using a slotted spoon, transfer salmon and asparagus to plate; cover and refrigerate until chilled, at least 30 minutes.

In small mixing bowl combine milk, sour cream, mayonnaise, horseradish, and capers; mix well. Serve as directed in microwave method.

Each serving provides: 3 Protein Exchanges; 2¾ Vegetable Exchanges; 1 Fat Exchange; 40 Optional Calories

Per serving: 259 calories; 26 g protein; 13 g fat; 9 g carbohydrate; 109 mg calcium; 191 mg sodium; 72 mg cholesterol; 2 g dietary fiber

Matzo Torte

Makes 4 servings

4 eggs
3 tablespoons whipped cream cheese
4 matzo boards (about 1 ounce each)
Water
½ cup *each* diced onion, celery, green bell pepper, and grated carrot

1 tablespoon plus 1 teaspoon peanut *or* vegetable oil
2 ounces *each* diced smoked salmon (lox) and Muenster cheese, shredded

Microwave Method: In blender container combine eggs and cream cheese and process until combined; set aside. In 8 × 8 × 2-inch microwavable baking dish arrange matzos; add water to cover and let soak for 1 minute. Remove matzos and any remaining liquid; drain matzos and set aside on sheet of paper towel.

In same baking dish combine vegetables and oil; stir well to thoroughly combine. Microwave on High (100%) for 6 minutes, stirring once halfway through cooking. Add salmon and stir to combine; remove vegetable-salmon mixture and set aside.

In same baking dish arrange 1 matzo board; top with ⅓ of the vegetable-salmon mixture and ½ ounce Muenster cheese. Repeat procedure 2 more times; set remaining matzo in baking dish and sprinkle with remaining ½ ounce Muenster cheese. Pour egg mixture evenly over torte, pressing top of torte down slightly. Microwave on High for 8 minutes, rotating dish ½ turn halfway through cooking. Let stand for 1 minute.

Conventional Method: Process eggs and cream cheese and soak matzos in water as directed in microwave method.

In 8-inch nonstick skillet heat oil; add vegetables and sauté over high heat, stirring frequently, until tender-crisp, about 5 minutes. Remove from heat; stir in salmon.

Preheat oven to 350°F. In 8 × 8 × 2-inch nonstick baking pan arrange matzos, vegetable-salmon mixture, Muenster cheese, and egg mixture as directed in microwave method. Bake until golden brown and egg mixture is set, about 30 minutes.

Each serving provides: 2 Protein Exchanges; 2 Bread Exchanges; 1 Vegetable Exchange; 1 Fat Exchange; 25 Optional Calories

Per serving: 342 calories; 16 g protein; 18 g fat; 29 g carbohydrate; 151 mg calcium; 315 mg sodium; 298 mg cholesterol; 1 g dietary fiber (this figure does not include matzo boards; nutrition analysis not available)

MAY

SUNDAY	MONDAY	TUESDAY	WEDNESDAY
		1	2
6	7	8	9
13	14	15	16
20	21	22	23
27	28	29	30

MAY

THURSDAY	FRIDAY	SATURDAY
3	4	5
10	11	12
17	18	19
24	25	26
31		

*Microwave
Menu
of the Month*

Strawberries sprinkled
with Confectioners'
Sugar

Spinach Frittata

Garden Salad with
Carrot Curls and French
Dressing

Blueberry Muffin with
Peach Preserves

Coffee or Tea

NOTES/GOALS

WEEKLY FOOD DIARY

	MONDAY	TUESDAY	WEDNESDAY	THURSDAY	FRIDAY	SATURDAY	SUNDAY
DAILY TOTALS	FRUIT ____ VEG ____ FAT ____ PROTEIN ____ BREAD ____ MILK ____ FLOATING ____		FRUIT ____ VEG ____ FAT ____ PROTEIN ____ BREAD ____ MILK ____ FLOATING ____	FRUIT ____ VEG ____ FAT ____ PROTEIN ____ BREAD ____ MILK ____ FLOATING ____	FRUIT ____ VEG ____ FAT ____ PROTEIN ____ BREAD ____ MILK ____ FLOATING ____	FRUIT ____ VEG ____ FAT ____ PROTEIN ____ BREAD ____ MILK ____ FLOATING ____	FRUIT ____ VEG ____ FAT ____ PROTEIN ____ BREAD ____ MILK ____ FLOATING ____
BREAKFAST							
LUNCH							
DINNER							
SNACKS							

WEEKLY LIMITS EGGS _____   CHEESE _____   MEAT _____   ORGAN MEAT _____   OPTIONAL CALORIES _____

I will attend my Weight Watchers meeting this week on _____

MONDAY
30

TUESDAY
1

WEDNESDAY
2

THURSDAY
3

FRIDAY
4

SATURDAY
5

SUNDAY
6

	S	M	T	W	T	F	S
		1	2	3	4	5	6	7
A	8	9	10	11	12	13	14
P	15	16	17	18	19	20	21
R	22	23	24	25	26	27	28
	29	30					

	S	M	T	W	T	F	S
			1	2	3	4	5
M	6	7	8	9	10	11	12
A	13	14	15	16	17	18	19
Y	20	21	22	23	24	25	26
	27	28	29	30	31		

	S	M	T	W	T	F	S
J						1	2
U	3	4	5	6	7	8	9
N	10	11	12	13	14	15	16
E	17	18	19	20	21	22	23
	24	25	26	27	28	29	30

WEEKLY FOOD DIARY

	MONDAY	TUESDAY	WEDNESDAY	THURSDAY	FRIDAY	SATURDAY	SUNDAY
DAILY TOTALS	FRUIT ____ VEG ____ FAT ____ PROTEIN ____ BREAD ____ MILK ____ FLOATING ____	FRUIT ____ VEG ____ FAT ____ PROTEIN ____ BREAD ____ MILK ____ FLOATING ____	FRUIT ____ VEG ____ FAT ____ PROTEIN ____ BREAD ____ MILK ____ FLOATING ____	FRUIT ____ VEG ____ FAT ____ PROTEIN ____ BREAD ____ MILK ____ FLOATING ____	FRUIT ____ VEG ____ FAT ____ PROTEIN ____ BREAD ____ MILK ____ FLOATING ____	FRUIT ____ VEG ____ FAT ____ PROTEIN ____ BREAD ____ MILK ____ FLOATING ____	FRUIT ____ VEG ____ FAT ____ PROTEIN ____ BREAD ____ MILK ____ FLOATING ____
BREAKFAST							
LUNCH							
DINNER							
SNACKS							

WEEKLY LIMITS   EGGS _____   CHEESE _____   MEAT _____   ORGAN MEAT _____   OPTIONAL CALORIES _____

I will attend my Weight Watchers meeting this week on _____

MONDAY
7

TUESDAY
8

WEDNESDAY
9

THURSDAY
10

FRIDAY
11

SATURDAY
12

Mother's Day

SUNDAY
13

	S	M	T	W	T	F	S
		1	2	3	4	5	6	7
A	8	9	10	11	12	13	14
P	15	16	17	18	19	20	21
R	22	23	24	25	26	27	28
	29	30					

	S	M	T	W	T	F	S
			1	2	3	4	5
M	6	7	8	9	10	11	12
A	13	14	15	16	17	18	19
Y	20	21	22	23	24	25	26
	27	28	29	30	31		

	S	M	T	W	T	F	S
						1	2
J	3	4	5	6	7	8	9
U	10	11	12	13	14	15	16
N	17	18	19	20	21	22	23
E	24	25	26	27	28	29	30

WEEKLY FOOD DIARY

	MONDAY	TUESDAY	WEDNESDAY	THURSDAY	FRIDAY	SATURDAY	SUNDAY
DAILY TOTALS	FRUIT ____ VEG ____ FAT ____ PROTEIN ____ BREAD ____ MILK ____ FLOATING ____	FRUIT ____ VEG ____ FAT ____ PROTEIN ____ BREAD ____ MILK ____ FLOATING ____	FRUIT ____ VEG ____ FAT ____ PROTEIN ____ BREAD ____ MILK ____ FLOATING ____	FRUIT ____ VEG ____ FAT ____ PROTEIN ____ BREAD ____ MILK ____ FLOATING ____	FRUIT ____ VEG ____ FAT ____ PROTEIN ____ BREAD ____ MILK ____ FLOATING ____	FRUIT ____ VEG ____ FAT ____ PROTEIN ____ BREAD ____ MILK ____ FLOATING ____	FRUIT ____ VEG ____ FAT ____ PROTEIN ____ BREAD ____ MILK ____ FLOATING ____
BREAKFAST							
LUNCH							
DINNER							
SNACKS							

WEEKLY LIMITS   EGGS ____   CHEESE ____   MEAT ____   ORGAN MEAT ____   OPTIONAL CALORIES ____

I will attend my Weight Watchers meeting this week on _____

ENGAGEMENTS

MAY

1 9 9 0

MONDAY
14

Weight Watchers 27th Anniversary

TUESDAY
15

WEDNESDAY
16

THURSDAY
17

FRIDAY
18

Armed Forces Day

SATURDAY
19

SUNDAY
20

	S	M	T	W	T	F	S
		1	2	3	4	5	6	7
A	8	9	10	11	12	13	14
P	15	16	17	18	19	20	21
R	22	23	24	25	26	27	28
	29	30					

	S	M	T	W	T	F	S
			1	2	3	4	5
M	6	7	8	9	10	11	12
A	13	14	15	16	17	18	19
Y	20	21	22	23	24	25	26
	27	28	29	30	31		

	S	M	T	W	T	F	S
J						1	2
U	3	4	5	6	7	8	9
N	10	11	12	13	14	15	16
E	17	18	19	20	21	22	23
	24	25	26	27	28	29	30

WEEKLY FOOD DIARY

	MONDAY	TUESDAY	WEDNESDAY	THURSDAY	FRIDAY	SATURDAY	SUNDAY
DAILY TOTALS	FRUIT ____ VEG ____ FAT ____ PROTEIN ____ BREAD ____ MILK ____ FLOATING ____	FRUIT ____ VEG ____ FAT ____ PROTEIN ____ BREAD ____ MILK ____ FLOATING ____	FRUIT ____ VEG ____ FAT ____ PROTEIN ____ BREAD ____ MILK ____ FLOATING ____	FRUIT ____ VEG ____ FAT ____ PROTEIN ____ BREAD ____ MILK ____ FLOATING ____	FRUIT ____ VEG ____ FAT ____ PROTEIN ____ BREAD ____ MILK ____ FLOATING ____	FRUIT ____ VEG ____ FAT ____ PROTEIN ____ BREAD ____ MILK ____ FLOATING ____	FRUIT ____ VEG ____ FAT ____ PROTEIN ____ BREAD ____ MILK ____ FLOATING ____
BREAKFAST							
LUNCH							
DINNER							
SNACKS							

WEEKLY LIMITS   EGGS ____   CHEESE ____   MEAT ____   ORGAN MEAT ____   OPTIONAL CALORIES ____

I will attend my Weight Watchers meeting this week on _____

Victoria Day (Canada)

MONDAY
21

TUESDAY
22

WEDNESDAY
23

THURSDAY
24

FRIDAY
25

SATURDAY
26

SUNDAY
27

	S	M	T	W	T	F	S
	1	2	3	4	5	6	7
A	8	9	10	11	12	13	14
P	15	16	17	18	19	20	21
R	22	23	24	25	26	27	28
	29	30					

	S	M	T	W	T	F	S
			1	2	3	4	5
M	6	7	8	9	10	11	12
A	13	14	15	16	17	18	19
Y	20	21	22	23	24	25	26
	27	28	29	30	31		

	S	M	T	W	T	F	S
J						1	2
U	3	4	5	6	7	8	9
N	10	11	12	13	14	15	16
E	17	18	19	20	21	22	23
	24	25	26	27	28	29	30

WEEKLY FOOD DIARY

	MONDAY	TUESDAY	WEDNESDAY	THURSDAY	FRIDAY	SATURDAY	SUNDAY
DAILY TOTALS	FRUIT ____ VEG ____ FAT ____ PROTEIN ____ BREAD ____ MILK ____ FLOATING ____	FRUIT ____ VEG ____ FAT ____ PROTEIN ____ BREAD ____ MILK ____ FLOATING ____	FRUIT ____ VEG ____ FAT ____ PROTEIN ____ BREAD ____ MILK ____ FLOATING ____	FRUIT ____ VEG ____ FAT ____ PROTEIN ____ BREAD ____ MILK ____ FLOATING ____	FRUIT ____ VEG ____ FAT ____ PROTEIN ____ BREAD ____ MILK ____ FLOATING ____	FRUIT ____ VEG ____ FAT ____ PROTEIN ____ BREAD ____ MILK ____ FLOATING ____	FRUIT ____ VEG ____ FAT ____ PROTEIN ____ BREAD ____ MILK ____ FLOATING ____
BREAKFAST							
LUNCH							
DINNER							
SNACKS							

WEEKLY LIMITS EGGS ____ CHEESE ____ MEAT ____ ORGAN MEAT ____ OPTIONAL CALORIES ____

I will attend my Weight Watchers meeting this week on ____

MAY
JUNE

1990

Memorial Day (observed)

MONDAY
28

TUESDAY
29

Memorial Day

WEDNESDAY
30

THURSDAY
31

FRIDAY
1

SATURDAY
2

SUNDAY
3

	S	M	T	W	T	F	S
		1	2	3	4	5	6	7
A	8	9	10	11	12	13	14
P	15	16	17	18	19	20	21
R	22	23	24	25	26	27	28
	29	30					

	S	M	T	W	T	F	S
			1	2	3	4	5
M	6	7	8	9	10	11	12
A	13	14	15	16	17	18	19
Y	20	21	22	23	24	25	26
	27	28	29	30	31		

	S	M	T	W	T	F	S
						1	2
J	3	4	5	6	7	8	9
U	10	11	12	13	14	15	16
N	17	18	19	20	21	22	23
E	24	25	26	27	28	29	30

Oriental Chicken Soup

Makes 2 servings, about 2 cups each

½ cup *each* diagonally thinly sliced scallions (green onions) and celery
1½ teaspoons peanut *or* vegetable oil
2 cups water
3 ounces skinned and boned chicken breasts, cut into thin strips
2 teaspoons dry sherry

1 packet instant chicken broth and seasoning mix
1 teaspoon reduced-sodium soy sauce
½ teaspoon Chinese sesame oil
2 cups chopped bok choy (Chinese cabbage)

Microwave Method: In 2-quart microwavable casserole combine scallions, celery, and peanut (or vegetable) oil; stir well to thoroughly combine. Microwave on High (100%) for 30 seconds. Add remaining ingredients except bok choy and stir to combine. Cover with vented plastic wrap and microwave on High for 3 minutes, stirring soup halfway through cooking. Stir in bok choy; replace plastic wrap and let stand for 2 minutes, until bok choy is tender-crisp and chicken is tender.

Conventional Method: In 2-quart saucepan heat peanut (or vegetable) oil; add scallions and celery and sauté until tender-crisp, about 2 minutes. Add remaining ingredients except bok choy; stir to combine and bring to a boil. Reduce heat to low, partially cover, and let simmer until flavors blend, about 5 minutes. Remove from heat and stir in bok choy; cover tightly and let stand until bok choy is tender-crisp and chicken is tender, about 5 minutes.

Each serving provides: 1 Protein Exchange; 3 Vegetable Exchanges; 1 Fat Exchange; 10 Optional Calories

Per serving: 123 calories; 12 g protein; 5 g fat; 6 g carbohydrate; 90 mg calcium; 658 mg sodium; 25 mg cholesterol; 6 g dietary fiber

Hot German Potato Salad

Makes 2 servings

9 ounces cooked new red potatoes, sliced (hot)
2 slices crisp bacon, crumbled
2 tablespoons chopped onion
2 teaspoons vegetable oil
1 teaspoon all-purpose flour

¼ cup *each* canned ready-to-serve chicken broth and red wine vinegar
1 teaspoon chopped fresh parsley
¼ teaspoon granulated sugar
Dash *each* salt and white pepper

Microwave Method: In small mixing bowl combine potatoes and bacon; set aside.

In small microwavable mixing bowl combine onion and oil; microwave on High (100%) for 1 minute until softened. Sprinkle flour over onion and stir quickly to combine; stir in broth, vinegar, parsley, sugar, salt, and pepper. Microwave on High for 1 minute until mixture thickens. Pour onion mixture over potato mixture; stir thoroughly to combine and serve immediately.

Conventional Method: In small mixing bowl combine potatoes and bacon; set aside.

In 8-inch nonstick skillet heat oil over medium-high heat; add onion and sauté until onion is softened, 1 to 2 minutes. Sprinkle flour over onion and stir quickly to combine. Continuing to stir, gradually add broth, vinegar, parsley, sugar, salt, and pepper; cook, stirring occasionally, until mixture thickens, 3 to 4 minutes. Pour onion mixture over potato mixture; stir thoroughly to combine and serve immediately.

Each serving provides: 1½ Bread Exchanges; ⅛ Vegetable Exchange; 1 Fat Exchange; 55 Optional Calories

Per serving: 205 calories; 5 g protein; 8 g fat; 29 g carbohydrate; 15 mg calcium; 299 mg sodium; 5 mg cholesterol; 3 g dietary fiber

Spinach Frittata

Makes 4 servings

4 eggs
½ cup evaporated skimmed milk
¼ pound domestic provolone cheese, shredded, divided
1 tablespoon chopped fresh Italian (flat-leaf) parsley

⅛ teaspoon *each* garlic powder, ground nutmeg, salt, and pepper
½ cup well-drained cooked spinach leaves

Microwave Method: Using a wire whisk, in medium mixing bowl combine eggs, milk, 3 ounces cheese, the parsley, and seasonings and beat until thoroughly combined; add spinach and stir to combine. Spray 7-inch microwavable pie plate with nonstick cooking spray; pour spinach mixture into plate. Microwave on Medium-High (70%) for 2 minutes, stirring with rubber scraper halfway through cooking. Microwave on Medium (50%) for 3 minutes, stirring every 45 seconds. Top with remaining 1 ounce cheese. Microwave on Low (30%) for 5 minutes, rotating dish ½ turn after 2½ minutes. Let frittata stand for 2 minutes.

Conventional Method: Preheat oven to 350°F. Using a wire whisk, in medium mixing bowl combine eggs, milk, 3 ounces cheese, the parsley, and seasonings and beat until thoroughly combined; add spinach and stir to combine. Spray 7-inch pie plate with nonstick cooking spray; pour spinach mixture into plate and sprinkle with remaining 1 ounce cheese. Bake for 40 minutes (until a knife, inserted in center, comes out clean).

Each serving provides: 2 Protein Exchanges; ¼ Vegetable Exchange; ¼ Milk Exchange
Per serving: 210 calories; 16 g protein; 13 g fat; 6 g carbohydrate; 368 mg calcium; 440 mg sodium; 295 mg cholesterol; 0.5 g dietary fiber

Custard with Raspberry Topping

Makes 2 servings

½ cup *each* evaporated skimmed milk and whole milk
1 egg
2 tablespoons plus 2 teaspoons instant nonfat dry milk powder

1 teaspoon *each* granulated sugar and vanilla extract
½ cup raspberries
1 tablespoon raspberry syrup

Microwave Method: Using a wire whisk, in medium mixing bowl combine all ingredients except raspberries and syrup and beat until combined. Spray two 10-ounce microwavable custard cups with nonstick cooking spray and pour half of the egg mixture into each cup. Set cups in 8 × 8 × 2-inch microwavable baking dish; pour water into dish to a depth of about 1 inch and microwave on Medium (50%) for 17 minutes (until a knife, inserted in center, comes out clean). Let stand for 1 minute. Remove cups from water bath; let custard stand at room temperature for 5 minutes. Cover and refrigerate until chilled, about 30 minutes.

To serve, onto each of 2 serving plates invert each custard; top each with half of the raspberries and then drizzle berries with half of the syrup.

Conventional Method: Preheat oven to 350°F. Using a wire whisk, in medium mixing bowl combine all ingredients except raspberries and syrup and beat until combined. Spray two 10-ounce custard cups with nonstick cooking spray and pour half of the egg mixture into each cup. Set cups in 8 × 8 × 2-inch baking pan; pour water into pan to a depth of about 1 inch and bake for 40 to 45 minutes (until a knife, inserted in center, comes out clean). Remove cups from water bath; let custard stand at room temperature for 5 minutes. Cover and refrigerate until chilled, about 30 minutes.

To serve, onto each of 2 serving plates invert each custard; top each with half of the raspberries and then drizzle berries with half of the syrup.

Each serving provides: ½ Protein Exchange; ½ Fruit Exchange; 1 Milk Exchange; 55 Optional Calories
Per serving: 202 calories; 12 g protein; 5 g fat; 26 g carbohydrate; 348 mg calcium; 169 mg sodium; 149 mg cholesterol; 1 g dietary fiber

JUNE

SUNDAY	MONDAY	TUESDAY	WEDNESDAY
3	4	5	6
10	11	12	13
17	18	19	20
24	25	26	27

JUNE

THURSDAY	FRIDAY	SATURDAY
	1	2
7	8	9
14	15	16
21	22	23
28	29	30

Microwave Menu of the Month

Chilled Tiny Shrimp on Lettuce with Seafood Cocktail Sauce and Lemon Wedge

Scrambled Eggs Deluxe

Toasted Bagel with Margarine

Mock Mimosa (chilled orange juice with club soda and mint sprig)

NOTES/GOALS

WEEKLY FOOD DIARY

	MONDAY	TUESDAY	WEDNESDAY	THURSDAY	FRIDAY	SATURDAY	SUNDAY
DAILY TOTALS	FRUIT ___ VEG ___ FAT ___ PROTEIN ___ BREAD ___ MILK ___ FLOATING ___	FRUIT ___ VEG ___ FAT ___ PROTEIN ___ BREAD ___ MILK ___ FLOATING ___	FRUIT ___ VEG ___ FAT ___ PROTEIN ___ BREAD ___ MILK ___ FLOATING ___	FRUIT ___ VEG ___ FAT ___ PROTEIN ___ BREAD ___ MILK ___ FLOATING ___	FRUIT ___ VEG ___ FAT ___ PROTEIN ___ BREAD ___ MILK ___ FLOATING ___	FRUIT ___ VEG ___ FAT ___ PROTEIN ___ BREAD ___ MILK ___ FLOATING ___	FRUIT ___ VEG ___ FAT ___ PROTEIN ___ BREAD ___ MILK ___ FLOATING ___
BREAKFAST							
LUNCH							
DINNER							
SNACKS							

WEEKLY LIMITS   EGGS ___   CHEESE ___   MEAT ___   ORGAN MEAT ___   OPTIONAL CALORIES ___

I will attend my Weight Watchers meeting this week on ___

JUNE

1 9 9 0

MONDAY
4

TUESDAY
5

WEDNESDAY
6

THURSDAY
7

FRIDAY
8

SATURDAY
9

SUNDAY
10

	S	M	T	W	T	F	S
			1	2	3	4	5
M	6	7	8	9	10	11	12
A	13	14	15	16	17	18	19
Y	20	21	22	23	24	25	26
	27	28	29	30	31		

	S	M	T	W	T	F	S
J						1	2
U	3	4	5	6	7	8	9
N	10	11	12	13	14	15	16
E	17	18	19	20	21	22	23
	24	25	26	27	28	29	30

	S	M	T	W	T	F	S
J	1	2	3	4	5	6	7
U	8	9	10	11	12	13	14
L	15	16	17	18	19	20	21
Y	22	23	24	25	26	27	28
	29	30	31				

WEEKLY FOOD DIARY

	MONDAY	TUESDAY	WEDNESDAY	THURSDAY	FRIDAY	SATURDAY	SUNDAY
DAILY TOTALS	FRUIT ____ VEG ____ FAT ____ PROTEIN ____ BREAD ____ MILK ____ FLOATING ____	FRUIT ____ VEG ____ FAT ____ PROTEIN ____ BREAD ____ MILK ____ FLOATING ____	FRUIT ____ VEG ____ FAT ____ PROTEIN ____ BREAD ____ MILK ____ FLOATING ____	FRUIT ____ VEG ____ FAT ____ PROTEIN ____ BREAD ____ MILK ____ FLOATING ____	FRUIT ____ VEG ____ FAT ____ PROTEIN ____ BREAD ____ MILK ____ FLOATING ____	FRUIT ____ VEG ____ FAT ____ PROTEIN ____ BREAD ____ MILK ____ FLOATING ____	FRUIT ____ VEG ____ FAT ____ PROTEIN ____ BREAD ____ MILK ____ FLOATING ____
BREAKFAST							
LUNCH							
DINNER							
SNACKS							

WEEKLY LIMITS EGGS ____ CHEESE ____ MEAT ____ ORGAN MEAT ____ OPTIONAL CALORIES ____

I will attend my Weight Watchers meeting this week on _____

E N G A G E M E N T S

JUNE

1 9 9 0

MONDAY
11

TUESDAY
12

WEDNESDAY
13

Flag Day

THURSDAY
14

FRIDAY
15

SATURDAY
16

Father's Day

SUNDAY
17

	S	M	T	W	T	F	S
			1	2	3	4	5
M	6	7	8	9	10	11	12
A	13	14	15	16	17	18	19
Y	20	21	22	23	24	25	26
	27	28	29	30	31		

	S	M	T	W	T	F	S
						1	2
J	3	4	5	6	7	8	9
U	10	11	12	13	14	15	16
N	17	18	19	20	21	22	23
E	24	25	26	27	28	29	30

	S	M	T	W	T	F	S
	1	2	3	4	5	6	7
J	8	9	10	11	12	13	14
U	15	16	17	18	19	20	21
L	22	23	24	25	26	27	28
Y	29	30	31				

WEEKLY FOOD DIARY

	MONDAY	TUESDAY	WEDNESDAY	THURSDAY	FRIDAY	SATURDAY	SUNDAY
DAILY TOTALS	FRUIT ____ VEG ____ FAT ____ PROTEIN ____ BREAD ____ MILK ____ FLOATING ____	FRUIT ____ VEG ____ FAT ____ PROTEIN ____ BREAD ____ MILK ____ FLOATING ____	FRUIT ____ VEG ____ FAT ____ PROTEIN ____ BREAD ____ MILK ____ FLOATING ____	FRUIT ____ VEG ____ FAT ____ PROTEIN ____ BREAD ____ MILK ____ FLOATING ____	FRUIT ____ VEG ____ FAT ____ PROTEIN ____ BREAD ____ MILK ____ FLOATING ____	FRUIT ____ VEG ____ FAT ____ PROTEIN ____ BREAD ____ MILK ____ FLOATING ____	FRUIT ____ VEG ____ FAT ____ PROTEIN ____ BREAD ____ MILK ____ FLOATING ____
BREAKFAST							
LUNCH							
DINNER							
SNACKS							

WEEKLY LIMITS   EGGS ____   CHEESE ____   MEAT ____   ORGAN MEAT ____   OPTIONAL CALORIES ____

I will attend my Weight Watchers meeting this week on _____

JUNE

1 9 9 0

MONDAY
18

TUESDAY
19

WEDNESDAY
20

THURSDAY
21

FRIDAY
22

SATURDAY
23

SUNDAY
24

	S	M	T	W	T	F	S
			1	2	3	4	5
M	6	7	8	9	10	11	12
A	13	14	15	16	17	18	19
Y	20	21	22	23	24	25	26
	27	28	29	30	31		

	S	M	T	W	T	F	S
						1	2
J	3	4	5	6	7	8	9
U	10	11	12	13	14	15	16
N	17	18	19	20	21	22	23
E	24	25	26	27	28	29	30

	S	M	T	W	T	F	S
	1	2	3	4	5	6	7
J	8	9	10	11	12	13	14
U	15	16	17	18	19	20	21
L	22	23	24	25	26	27	28
Y	29	30	31				

WEEKLY FOOD DIARY

	MONDAY	TUESDAY	WEDNESDAY	THURSDAY	FRIDAY	SATURDAY	SUNDAY
DAILY TOTALS	FRUIT ___ VEG ___ FAT ___ PROTEIN ___ BREAD ___ MILK ___ FLOATING ___	FRUIT ___ VEG ___ FAT ___ PROTEIN ___ BREAD ___ MILK ___ FLOATING ___	FRUIT ___ VEG ___ FAT ___ PROTEIN ___ BREAD ___ MILK ___ FLOATING ___	FRUIT ___ VEG ___ FAT ___ PROTEIN ___ BREAD ___ MILK ___ FLOATING ___	FRUIT ___ VEG ___ FAT ___ PROTEIN ___ BREAD ___ MILK ___ FLOATING ___	FRUIT ___ VEG ___ FAT ___ PROTEIN ___ BREAD ___ MILK ___ FLOATING ___	FRUIT ___ VEG ___ FAT ___ PROTEIN ___ BREAD ___ MILK ___ FLOATING ___
BREAKFAST							
LUNCH							
DINNER							
SNACKS							

WEEKLY LIMITS EGGS ___   CHEESE ___   MEAT ___   ORGAN MEAT ___   OPTIONAL CALORIES ___

I will attend my Weight Watchers meeting this week on _____

MONDAY
25

TUESDAY
26

WEDNESDAY
27

THURSDAY
28

FRIDAY
29

SATURDAY
30

Canada Day (Canada)

SUNDAY
1

	S	M	T	W	T	F	S
			1	2	3	4	5
M	6	7	8	9	10	11	12
A	13	14	15	16	17	18	19
Y	20	21	22	23	24	25	26
	27	28	29	30	31		

	S	M	T	W	T	F	S
						1	2
J	3	4	5	6	7	8	9
U	10	11	12	13	14	15	16
N	17	18	19	20	21	22	23
E	24	25	26	27	28	29	30

	S	M	T	W	T	F	S
	1	2	3	4	5	6	7
J	8	9	10	11	12	13	14
U	15	16	17	18	19	20	21
L	22	23	24	25	26	27	28
Y	29	30	31				

WEIGHT
RECIPE
WATCHERS

Scrambled Eggs Deluxe

Makes 2 servings

1 tablespoon whipped butter
1 cup sliced mushrooms
½ cup *each* diced onion and celery
2 eggs

¼ cup skim *or* nonfat milk
Dash *each* salt and pepper
2 teaspoons grated Parmesan cheese

Microwave Method: In 8-inch microwavable pie plate microwave butter on High (100%) for 30 seconds until melted; add vegetables and stir well to thoroughly combine. Microwave on High for 4 minutes, stirring halfway through cooking. Using a wire whisk, in small mixing bowl combine eggs, milk, salt, and pepper and beat until combined; stir into vegetable mixture. Microwave on High for 2 minutes, stirring egg mixture toward center of plate halfway through cooking. Sprinkle with cheese and let stand for 1 minute.

Conventional Method: In 8-inch nonstick skillet melt butter; add vegetables and sauté over medium-high heat until tender-crisp, about 5 minutes. While vegetables are cooking, prepare eggs. Using a wire whisk, in small mixing bowl combine eggs, milk, salt, and pepper and beat until combined. Pour egg mixture into skillet over vegetables and cook over medium heat, stirring frequently, until eggs are set, about 5 minutes. Sprinkle with cheese and serve.

Each serving provides: 1 Protein Exchange; 2 Vegetable Exchanges; 45 Optional Calories

Per serving: 150 calories; 9 g protein; 9 g fat; 8 g carbohydrate; 113 mg calcium; 240 mg sodium; 284 mg cholesterol; 1 g dietary fiber

Shrimp with Honey-Mustard Dipping Sauce

Makes 2 servings

1 dozen large shrimp, peeled and
  deveined*
Water
3 peppercorns
1 lemon slice (1 inch thick)
1 bay leaf

1½ cups ice cubes
2 teaspoons *each* chopped scallion
  (green onion), Dijon-style mustard,
  freshly squeezed lemon juice, and
  honey

Microwave Method: In 1-quart microwavable casserole combine shrimp, 1 cup water, the peppercorns, lemon slice, and bay leaf. Cover with vented plastic wrap and microwave on High (100%) for 1½ minutes. Turn shrimp over and rearrange in casserole, moving those that have been in the center to the edge. Replace vented plastic wrap and microwave on High for 45 seconds to 1 minute until shrimp turn pink. Remove plastic wrap and drain shrimp; immediately add ice to stop the cooking process. Let stand for 2 minutes. Drain shrimp, discarding any unmelted ice, the peppercorns, lemon slice, and bay leaf; set aside.

Using a fork, in small microwavable serving bowl combine 2 teaspoons water, the scallion, mustard, lemon juice, and honey, stirring to combine. Microwave on High for 30 seconds. Arrange shrimp over edge of serving bowl and serve.

Conventional Method: In 2-quart saucepan combine 3 cups water, the peppercorns, lemon slice, and bay leaf; cover and cook over high heat until mixture comes to a boil. Add shrimp, return mixture to a boil, and cook uncovered until shrimp turn pink, about 1 minute. Drain shrimp; immediately add ice to stop the cooking process. Let stand for 2 minutes. Drain shrimp, discarding any unmelted ice, the peppercorns, lemon slice, and bay leaf; set aside.

In small saucepan combine 2 teaspoons water, the scallion, mustard, lemon juice, and honey and cook over medium heat, stirring occasionally with a fork, until warm. Transfer to small serving bowl; arrange shrimp over edge of serving bowl and serve.

Each serving provides: 2 Protein Exchanges; 20 Optional Calories

Per serving: 85 calories; 12 g protein; 1 g fat; 7 g carbohydrate; 24 mg calcium; 278 mg sodium; 111 mg cholesterol; 0.1 g dietary fiber

* One dozen large shrimp will yield about ¼ pound cooked, peeled, and deveined seafood.

WEIGHT
RECIPE
WATCHERS

Chicken with Snow Peas and Sprouts

Makes 2 servings

¼ cup dry white table wine
2 tablespoons reduced-sodium soy sauce
1 tablespoon white wine vinegar
2 teaspoons Chinese sesame oil
1 garlic clove, minced

½ pound skinned and boned chicken breasts, cut into 2 × ½-inch strips
1 cup bean sprouts, rinsed and drained
¾ cup Chinese pea pods (snow peas), stem ends and strings removed
½ teaspoon sesame seed

Microwave Method: In medium glass or stainless-steel bowl combine wine, soy sauce, vinegar, oil, and garlic; add chicken and turn to coat. Cover with plastic wrap and refrigerate for at least 30 minutes.

In 10 × 6-inch microwavable baking dish arrange bean sprouts; top with chicken mixture. Cover with vented plastic wrap and microwave on High (100%) for 1 minute. Stir chicken and sprout mixture; top with Chinese pea pods. Replace vented plastic wrap and microwave on High for 4 minutes; let stand for 2 minutes. Sprinkle with sesame seed.

Conventional Method: In medium glass or stainless-steel bowl combine wine, soy sauce, vinegar, oil, and garlic; add chicken and turn to coat. Cover with plastic wrap and refrigerate for at least 30 minutes. Drain chicken, reserving marinade.

Heat 12-inch nonstick skillet; add chicken and cook over medium-high heat, stirring occasionally, for 2 minutes. Add bean sprouts and Chinese pea pods and sauté for 1 minute. Add reserved marinade mixture; increase heat to high and sauté until Chinese pea pods are tender-crisp, 2 to 3 minutes. Transfer to serving platter and sprinkle with sesame seed.

Each serving provides: 3 Protein Exchanges; 1¾ Vegetable Exchanges; 1 Fat Exchange; 35 Optional Calories

Per serving: 240 calories; 30 g protein; 7 g fat; 10 g carbohydrate; 58 mg calcium; 681 mg sodium; 66 mg cholesterol; 2 g dietary fiber

Seasoned Green Beans

Makes 2 servings

½ cup diced onion
2 teaspoons olive *or* vegetable oil
1 small garlic clove, minced
2 cups whole green beans, cut into 3-inch pieces
2 tablespoons water
1 teaspoon lemon juice

Dash *each* salt, pepper, and oregano leaves
1 medium tomato, diced
1 tablespoon *each* grated Parmesan cheese and chopped Italian (flat-leaf) parsley

Microwave Method: In 1-quart microwavable casserole combine onion, oil, and garlic; stir well to thoroughly combine. Cover with vented plastic wrap and microwave on High (100%) for 2 minutes. Add remaining ingredients except tomato, cheese, and parsley and stir to combine. Cover with vented plastic wrap and microwave on High for 4 minutes, stirring halfway through cooking. Add tomato and stir to combine; replace vented plastic wrap and microwave on High for 30 seconds. Sprinkle with cheese and parsley; let stand for 1 minute.

Conventional Method: In 10-inch skillet heat oil; add onion and garlic and sauté over medium heat until onion is lightly browned, about 2 minutes. Add remaining ingredients except tomato, cheese, and parsley and stir to combine. Reduce heat to low, cover, and let simmer until beans are tender, about 10 minutes. Add tomato and stir to combine; cover and let simmer 5 minutes longer. Transfer to serving platter; sprinkle with cheese and parsley.

Each serving provides: 3½ Vegetable Exchanges; 1 Fat Exchange; 15 Optional Calories

Per serving: 159 calories; 4 g protein; 6 g fat; 25 g carbohydrate; 116 mg calcium; 216 mg sodium; 2 mg cholesterol; 4 g dietary fiber

JULY

SUNDAY	MONDAY	TUESDAY	WEDNESDAY
1	2	3	4
8	9	10	11
15	16	17	18
22	23	24	25
29	30	31	

JULY

THURSDAY	FRIDAY	SATURDAY
5	6	7
12	13	14
19	20	21
26	27	28

Microwave Menu of the Month

Broiled Hamburger with Ketchup and Sliced Red Onion in Pita

Corn on the Cob with Lemon-Chive Butter

Coleslaw

Tossed Salad with Red Wine Vinegar and Herbs

Watermelon Wedge

Iced Tea with Lemon Wedge

NOTES/GOALS

WEEKLY FOOD DIARY

	MONDAY	TUESDAY	WEDNESDAY	THURSDAY	FRIDAY	SATURDAY	SUNDAY
DAILY TOTALS	FRUIT ___ VEG ___ FAT ___ PROTEIN ___ BREAD ___ MILK ___ FLOATING ___	FRUIT ___ VEG ___ FAT ___ PROTEIN ___ BREAD ___ MILK ___ FLOATING ___	FRUIT ___ VEG ___ FAT ___ PROTEIN ___ BREAD ___ MILK ___ FLOATING ___	FRUIT ___ VEG ___ FAT ___ PROTEIN ___ BREAD ___ MILK ___ FLOATING ___	FRUIT ___ VEG ___ FAT ___ PROTEIN ___ BREAD ___ MILK ___ FLOATING ___	FRUIT ___ VEG ___ FAT ___ PROTEIN ___ BREAD ___ MILK ___ FLOATING ___	FRUIT ___ VEG ___ FAT ___ PROTEIN ___ BREAD ___ MILK ___ FLOATING ___
BREAKFAST							
LUNCH							
DINNER							
SNACKS							

WEEKLY LIMITS EGGS ___ CHEESE ___ MEAT ___ ORGAN MEAT ___ OPTIONAL CALORIES ___

I will attend my Weight Watchers meeting this week on ___

ENGAGEMENTS

JULY

1990

MONDAY

2

TUESDAY

3

Independence Day

WEDNESDAY

4

THURSDAY

5

FRIDAY

6

SATURDAY

7

SUNDAY

8

	S	M	T	W	T	F	S
JUNE						1	2
	3	4	5	6	7	8	9
	10	11	12	13	14	15	16
	17	18	19	20	21	22	23
	24	25	26	27	28	29	30

	S	M	T	W	T	F	S
JULY	1	2	3	4	5	6	7
	8	9	10	11	12	13	14
	15	16	17	18	19	20	21
	22	23	24	25	26	27	28
	29	30	31				

	S	M	T	W	T	F	S
AUG				1	2	3	4
	5	6	7	8	9	10	11
	12	13	14	15	16	17	18
	19	20	21	22	23	24	25
	26	27	28	29	30	31	

WEEKLY FOOD DIARY

	MONDAY	TUESDAY	WEDNESDAY	THURSDAY	FRIDAY	SATURDAY	SUNDAY
D A I L Y T O T A L S	FRUIT ___ VEG ___ FAT ___ PROTEIN ___ BREAD ___ MILK ___ FLOATING ___	FRUIT ___ VEG ___ FAT ___ PROTEIN ___ BREAD ___ MILK ___ FLOATING ___	FRUIT ___ VEG ___ FAT ___ PROTEIN ___ BREAD ___ MILK ___ FLOATING ___	FRUIT ___ VEG ___ FAT ___ PROTEIN ___ BREAD ___ MILK ___ FLOATING ___	FRUIT ___ VEG ___ FAT ___ PROTEIN ___ BREAD ___ MILK ___ FLOATING ___	FRUIT ___ VEG ___ FAT ___ PROTEIN ___ BREAD ___ MILK ___ FLOATING ___	FRUIT ___ VEG ___ FAT ___ PROTEIN ___ BREAD ___ MILK ___ FLOATING ___
B R E A K F A S T							
L U N C H							
D I N N E R							
S N A C K S							

WEEKLY LIMITS   EGGS ___   CHEESE ___   MEAT ___   ORGAN MEAT ___   OPTIONAL CALORIES ___

I will attend my Weight Watchers meeting this week on _____

JULY

MONDAY
9

TUESDAY
10

WEDNESDAY
11

THURSDAY
12

FRIDAY
13

SATURDAY
14

SUNDAY
15

	S	M	T	W	T	F	S
JUNE						1	2
	3	4	5	6	7	8	9
	10	11	12	13	14	15	16
	17	18	19	20	21	22	23
	24	25	26	27	28	29	30

	S	M	T	W	T	F	S
JULY	1	2	3	4	5	6	7
	8	9	10	11	12	13	14
	15	16	17	18	19	20	21
	22	23	24	25	26	27	28
	29	30	31				

	S	M	T	W	T	F	S
AUG				1	2	3	4
	5	6	7	8	9	10	11
	12	13	14	15	16	17	18
	19	20	21	22	23	24	25
	26	27	28	29	30	31	

WEEKLY FOOD DIARY

	MONDAY	TUESDAY	WEDNESDAY	THURSDAY	FRIDAY	SATURDAY	SUNDAY
DAILY TOTALS	FRUIT ___ VEG ___ FAT ___ PROTEIN ___ BREAD ___ MILK ___ FLOATING ___	FRUIT ___ VEG ___ FAT ___ PROTEIN ___ BREAD ___ MILK ___ FLOATING ___	FRUIT ___ VEG ___ FAT ___ PROTEIN ___ BREAD ___ MILK ___ FLOATING ___	FRUIT ___ VEG ___ FAT ___ PROTEIN ___ BREAD ___ MILK ___ FLOATING ___	FRUIT ___ VEG ___ FAT ___ PROTEIN ___ BREAD ___ MILK ___ FLOATING ___	FRUIT ___ VEG ___ FAT ___ PROTEIN ___ BREAD ___ MILK ___ FLOATING ___	FRUIT ___ VEG ___ FAT ___ PROTEIN ___ BREAD ___ MILK ___ FLOATING ___
BREAKFAST							
LUNCH							
DINNER							
SNACKS							

WEEKLY LIMITS   EGGS ___   CHEESE ___   MEAT ___   ORGAN MEAT ___   OPTIONAL CALORIES ___

I will attend my Weight Watchers meeting this week on _____

ENGAGEMENTS

JULY

1 9 9 0

MONDAY
16

TUESDAY
17

WEDNESDAY
18

THURSDAY
19

FRIDAY
20

SATURDAY
21

SUNDAY
22

	S	M	T	W	T	F	S
JUNE						1	2
	3	4	5	6	7	8	9
	10	11	12	13	14	15	16
	17	18	19	20	21	22	23
	24	25	26	27	28	29	30

	S	M	T	W	T	F	S
JULY	1	2	3	4	5	6	7
	8	9	10	11	12	13	14
	15	16	17	18	19	20	21
	22	23	24	25	26	27	28
	29	30	31				

	S	M	T	W	T	F	S
AUG				1	2	3	4
	5	6	7	8	9	10	11
	12	13	14	15	16	17	18
	19	20	21	22	23	24	25
	26	27	28	29	30	31	

WEEKLY FOOD DIARY

	MONDAY	TUESDAY	WEDNESDAY	THURSDAY	FRIDAY	SATURDAY	SUNDAY
D A I L Y T O T A L S	FRUIT _____ VEG _____ FAT _____ PROTEIN _____ BREAD _____ MILK _____ FLOATING _____	FRUIT _____ VEG _____ FAT _____ PROTEIN _____ BREAD _____ MILK _____ FLOATING _____	FRUIT _____ VEG _____ FAT _____ PROTEIN _____ BREAD _____ MILK _____ FLOATING _____	FRUIT _____ VEG _____ FAT _____ PROTEIN _____ BREAD _____ MILK _____ FLOATING _____	FRUIT _____ VEG _____ FAT _____ PROTEIN _____ BREAD _____ MILK _____ FLOATING _____	FRUIT _____ VEG _____ FAT _____ PROTEIN _____ BREAD _____ MILK _____ FLOATING _____	FRUIT _____ VEG _____ FAT _____ PROTEIN _____ BREAD _____ MILK _____ FLOATING _____
BREAKFAST							
LUNCH							
DINNER							
SNACKS							

WEEKLY LIMITS EGGS _____ CHEESE _____ MEAT _____ ORGAN MEAT _____ OPTIONAL CALORIES _____

I will attend my Weight Watchers meeting this week on _____

JULY

1990

MONDAY
23

TUESDAY
24

WEDNESDAY
25

THURSDAY
26

FRIDAY
27

SATURDAY
28

SUNDAY
29

	S	M	T	W	T	F	S
JUNE						1	2
	3	4	5	6	7	8	9
	10	11	12	13	14	15	16
	17	18	19	20	21	22	23
	24	25	26	27	28	29	30

	S	M	T	W	T	F	S
JULY	1	2	3	4	5	6	7
	8	9	10	11	12	13	14
	15	16	17	18	19	20	21
	22	23	24	25	26	27	28
	29	30	31				

	S	M	T	W	T	F	S
AUG				1	2	3	4
	5	6	7	8	9	10	11
	12	13	14	15	16	17	18
	19	20	21	22	23	24	25
	26	27	28	29	30	31	

WEIGHT
RECIPE
WATCHERS

Corn on the Cob with Lemon-Chive Butter

Makes 2 servings

2 tablespoons whipped butter, softened
½ teaspoon *each* chopped chives and
**   freshly squeezed lemon juice**

¼ teaspoon grated lemon peel
Dash white pepper
2 small ears corn on the cob (with
**   husk)**

Microwave Method: In cup or small bowl combine butter, chives, lemon juice, lemon peel, and pepper; mix well. Cover and refrigerate until ready to serve.

Place corn in microwave oven, leaving space between ears. Microwave on High (100%) for 4 to 5 minutes, until corn is cooked through, turning corn over halfway through cooking.

To serve, wrap base end of each corn with paper towel and, holding towel-covered base, fold back leaves of husk, being careful of steam. Pull out corn silk and remove half of the husk from each corn. On serving platter arrange each corn, husk-side down, and top each with half of the butter mixture.

Conventional Method: In cup or small bowl combine butter, chives, lemon juice, lemon peel, and pepper; mix well. Cover and refrigerate until ready to serve.

Remove husk from corn. Fill 2-quart saucepan with water to a depth of about 1 inch; add corn and bring to a boil. Reduce heat to low, cover, and let simmer until tender, about 5 minutes.

To serve, on serving platter arrange corn and top each with half of the butter mixture.

Each serving provides: 1 Bread Exchange; 50 Optional Calories

Per serving: 129 calories; 3 g protein; 7 g fat; 17 g carbohydrate; 4 mg calcium; 72 mg sodium; 16 mg cholesterol; 1 g dietary fiber

Soy Fish Fillets

Makes 2 servings

2 tablespoons *each* **reduced-sodium soy sauce and water**
2 teaspoons honey

1 teaspoon cornstarch
2 flounder *or* **sole fillets (¼ pound each)**

Microwave Method: In microwavable cup or small bowl combine all ingredients except fish, stirring to dissolve cornstarch. Microwave on High (100%) for 1 minute until mixture thickens, stirring halfway through cooking.

On microwavable plate arrange fish fillets and brush both sides of each fillet with an equal amount of soy sauce mixture. Microwave on High for 2 minutes, rotating plate halfway through cooking, until fish flakes easily when tested with a fork.

Conventional Method: In small saucepan combine all ingredients except fish, stirring to dissolve cornstarch. Cook over medium-high heat, stirring constantly, until mixture comes to a boil. Reduce heat to low and let simmer, stirring occasionally, until mixture thickens, about 2 minutes.

Preheat broiler. On nonstick baking sheet arrange fish fillets; brush with half of the soy sauce mixture. Broil 2 to 3 minutes. Carefully turn fillets over and brush with remaining soy sauce mixture. Broil until fish flakes easily when tested with a fork, 2 to 3 minutes longer.

Each serving provides: 3 Protein Exchanges; 25 Optional Calories

Per serving: 139 calories; 22 g protein; 1 g fat; 9 g carbohydrate; 24 mg calcium; 692 mg sodium; 54 mg cholesterol; dietary fiber data not available

WEIGHT
RECIPE
WATCHERS

Feta-Topped Tomatoes on Spinach

Makes 2 servings

3 ounces feta cheese

2 tablespoons whipped cream cheese

3 large plum tomatoes, cut in half lengthwise

⅛ teaspoon *each* oregano leaves and pepper

2 tablespoons *each* minced red onion, red wine vinegar, and water

2 teaspoons *each* Dijon-style mustard and olive *or* vegetable oil

1½ teaspoons chopped Italian (flat-leaf) parsley

2 cups spinach leaves, thoroughly washed, drained, and shredded

Microwave Method: In small mixing bowl thoroughly combine cheeses. Top each tomato half with ⅙ of the cheese mixture, then sprinkle each with oregano and pepper. Set tomatoes in 1-quart microwavable casserole; cover with vented plastic wrap and microwave on Medium-High (70%) for 1 minute. Set aside.

In small microwavable bowl combine remaining ingredients except spinach; microwave on High (100%) for 30 seconds.

To serve, on serving platter arrange spinach; top with tomato halves and pour vinegar mixture evenly over tomatoes.

Conventional Method: Preheat oven to 350°F. In small mixing bowl thoroughly combine cheeses. Top each tomato half with ⅙ of the cheese mixture, then sprinkle each with oregano and pepper. Set tomatoes in 1-quart flameproof casserole and bake until heated through, about 5 minutes. Turn oven control to broil and broil until cheese mixture melts, about 2 minutes.

In small saucepan combine remaining ingredients except spinach and cook over medium-high heat until mixture begins to boil.

To serve, on serving platter arrange spinach; top with tomato halves and pour vinegar mixture evenly over tomatoes.

Each serving provides: 1½ Protein Exchanges; 3½ Vegetable Exchanges; 1 Fat Exchange; 35 Optional Calories

Per serving: 220 calories; 9 g protein; 17 g fat; 9 g carbohydrate; 268 mg calcium; 700 mg sodium; 47 mg cholesterol; 2 g dietary fiber

WEIGHT

RECIPE

WATCHERS

Tropical Fruit Topping

Makes 4 servings, about ¼ cup each

⅓ cup apricot nectar
¼ cup dry white table wine
1 teaspoon *each* quick-cooking tapioca, firmly packed light brown sugar, and margarine
½ medium banana (about 3 ounces), peeled and sliced

1 teaspoon freshly squeezed lemon juice
½ pitted small mango (about 6½ ounces), pared and diced

Microwave Method: In small microwavable mixing bowl combine nectar, wine, tapioca, sugar, and margarine; stir to combine and let stand 5 minutes. Microwave on High (100%) for 3 minutes until mixture thickens and tapioca turns clear; set aside.

In small bowl combine banana and lemon juice; toss to combine. Add banana and mango to tapioca mixture and stir to combine. Cover bowl with vented plastic wrap and microwave on High (100%) for 1 minute until fruits are heated through. Uncover and let stand for 5 minutes before serving.

Conventional Method: In 1-cup liquid measure combine nectar, wine, and tapioca; stir to combine and let stand for 5 minutes. In small bowl combine banana and lemon juice; toss to combine.

In small saucepan melt margarine; add banana and sauté over medium-high heat until lightly browned, 1 to 2 minutes. Using a slotted spoon, transfer banana mixture to a plate and set aside. Add tapioca mixture and sugar to saucepan and cook, stirring frequently, until mixture thickens and tapioca turns clear, 2 to 3 minutes. Return banana mixture to saucepan; add mango and cook, stirring occasionally, until fruits are heated through, about 1 minute. Transfer to small bowl and let stand for 5 minutes before serving.

Each serving provides: ¼ Fat Exchange; ¾ Fruit Exchange; 25 Optional Calories

Per serving: 71 calories; 0.4 g protein; 1 g fat; 14 g carbohydrate; 8 mg calcium; 14 mg sodium; 0 mg cholesterol; 0.6 g dietary fiber

Note: Topping can be stored in refrigerator in jar with tight-fitting cover for up to 1 week.

AUGUST

SUNDAY	MONDAY	TUESDAY	WEDNESDAY
			1
5	6	7	8
12	13	14	15
19	20	21	22
26	27	28	29

AUGUST

THURSDAY	FRIDAY	SATURDAY
2	3	4
9	10	11
16	17	18
23	24	25
30	31	

Microwave Menu of the Month

Chicken BBQ Style

Baked Potato with Sour Cream and Chopped Chives

Cooked Sliced Zucchini

Sliced Mushrooms and Cherry Tomatoes on Spinach Leaves with Italian Dressing

Iced Coffee

NOTES/GOALS

WEEKLY FOOD DIARY

	MONDAY	TUESDAY	WEDNESDAY	THURSDAY	FRIDAY	SATURDAY	SUNDAY
DAILY TOTALS	FRUIT ____ VEG ____ FAT ____ PROTEIN ____ BREAD ____ MILK ____ FLOATING ____	FRUIT ____ VEG ____ FAT ____ PROTEIN ____ BREAD ____ MILK ____ FLOATING ____	FRUIT ____ VEG ____ FAT ____ PROTEIN ____ BREAD ____ MILK ____ FLOATING ____	FRUIT ____ VEG ____ FAT ____ PROTEIN ____ BREAD ____ MILK ____ FLOATING ____	FRUIT ____ VEG ____ FAT ____ PROTEIN ____ BREAD ____ MILK ____ FLOATING ____	FRUIT ____ VEG ____ FAT ____ PROTEIN ____ BREAD ____ MILK ____ FLOATING ____	FRUIT ____ VEG ____ FAT ____ PROTEIN ____ BREAD ____ MILK ____ FLOATING ____
BREAKFAST							
LUNCH							
DINNER							
SNACKS							

WEEKLY LIMITS EGGS ____ CHEESE ____ MEAT ____ ORGAN MEAT ____ OPTIONAL CALORIES ____

I will attend my Weight Watchers meeting this week on ____

ENGAGEMENTS

JULY
AUGUST

1 9 9 0

MONDAY
30

TUESDAY
31

WEDNESDAY
1

THURSDAY
2

FRIDAY
3

SATURDAY
4

SUNDAY
5

JULY	S	M	T	W	T	F	S
	1	2	3	4	5	6	7
	8	9	10	11	12	13	14
	15	16	17	18	19	20	21
	22	23	24	25	26	27	28
	29	30	31				

AUG	S	M	T	W	T	F	S
				1	2	3	4
	5	6	7	8	9	10	11
	12	13	14	15	16	17	18
	19	20	21	22	23	24	25
	26	27	28	29	30	31	

SEPT	S	M	T	W	T	F	S
							1
	2	3	4	5	6	7	8
	9	10	11	12	13	14	15
	16	17	18	19	20	21	22
	23	24	25	26	27	28	29
	30						

WEEKLY FOOD DIARY

	MONDAY	TUESDAY	WEDNESDAY	THURSDAY	FRIDAY	SATURDAY	SUNDAY
DAILY TOTALS	FRUIT ___ VEG ___ FAT ___ PROTEIN ___ BREAD ___ MILK ___ FLOATING ___	FRUIT ___ VEG ___ FAT ___ PROTEIN ___ BREAD ___ MILK ___ FLOATING ___	FRUIT ___ VEG ___ FAT ___ PROTEIN ___ BREAD ___ MILK ___ FLOATING ___	FRUIT ___ VEG ___ FAT ___ PROTEIN ___ BREAD ___ MILK ___ FLOATING ___	FRUIT ___ VEG ___ FAT ___ PROTEIN ___ BREAD ___ MILK ___ FLOATING ___	FRUIT ___ VEG ___ FAT ___ PROTEIN ___ BREAD ___ MILK ___ FLOATING ___	FRUIT ___ VEG ___ FAT ___ PROTEIN ___ BREAD ___ MILK ___ FLOATING ___
BREAKFAST							
LUNCH							
DINNER							
SNACKS							

WEEKLY LIMITS   EGGS _____   CHEESE _____   MEAT _____   ORGAN MEAT _____   OPTIONAL CALORIES _____

I will attend my Weight Watchers meeting this week on _____

ENGAGEMENTS

AUGUST

1 9 9 0

MONDAY
6

TUESDAY
7

WEDNESDAY
8

THURSDAY
9

FRIDAY
10

SATURDAY
11

SUNDAY
12

	S	M	T	W	T	F	S
JULY	1	2	3	4	5	6	7
	8	9	10	11	12	13	14
	15	16	17	18	19	20	21
	22	23	24	25	26	27	28
	29	30	31				

	S	M	T	W	T	F	S
AUG				1	2	3	4
	5	6	7	8	9	10	11
	12	13	14	15	16	17	18
	19	20	21	22	23	24	25
	26	27	28	29	30	31	

	S	M	T	W	T	F	S
SEPT							1
	2	3	4	5	6	7	8
	9	10	11	12	13	14	15
	16	17	18	19	20	21	22
	23	24	25	26	27	28	29
	30						

WEEKLY FOOD DIARY

	MONDAY	TUESDAY	WEDNESDAY	THURSDAY	FRIDAY	SATURDAY	SUNDAY
DAILY TOTALS	FRUIT ____ VEG ____ FAT ____ PROTEIN ____ BREAD ____ MILK ____ FLOATING ____	FRUIT ____ VEG ____ FAT ____ PROTEIN ____ BREAD ____ MILK ____ FLOATING ____	FRUIT ____ VEG ____ FAT ____ PROTEIN ____ BREAD ____ MILK ____ FLOATING ____	FRUIT ____ VEG ____ FAT ____ PROTEIN ____ BREAD ____ MILK ____ FLOATING ____	FRUIT ____ VEG ____ FAT ____ PROTEIN ____ BREAD ____ MILK ____ FLOATING ____	FRUIT ____ VEG ____ FAT ____ PROTEIN ____ BREAD ____ MILK ____ FLOATING ____	FRUIT ____ VEG ____ FAT ____ PROTEIN ____ BREAD ____ MILK ____ FLOATING ____
BREAKFAST							
LUNCH							
DINNER							
SNACKS							

WEEKLY LIMITS   EGGS ____   CHEESE ____   MEAT ____   ORGAN MEAT ____   OPTIONAL CALORIES ____

I will attend my Weight Watchers meeting this week on ____

ENGAGEMENTS

AUGUST

1990

MONDAY
13

TUESDAY
14

WEDNESDAY
15

THURSDAY
16

FRIDAY
17

SATURDAY
18

SUNDAY
19

	S	M	T	W	T	F	S
J	1	2	3	4	5	6	7
U	8	9	10	11	12	13	14
L	15	16	17	18	19	20	21
Y	22	23	24	25	26	27	28
	29	30	31				

	S	M	T	W	T	F	S
				1	2	3	4
A	5	6	7	8	9	10	11
U	12	13	14	15	16	17	18
G	19	20	21	22	23	24	25
	26	27	28	29	30	31	

	S	M	T	W	T	F	S
							1
S	2	3	4	5	6	7	8
E	9	10	11	12	13	14	15
P	16	17	18	19	20	21	22
T	23	24	25	26	27	28	29
	30						

WEEKLY FOOD DIARY

	MONDAY	TUESDAY	WEDNESDAY	THURSDAY	FRIDAY	SATURDAY	SUNDAY
D A I L Y T O T A L S	FRUIT ——— VEG ——— FAT ——— PROTEIN ——— BREAD ——— MILK ——— FLOATING ———	FRUIT ——— VEG ——— FAT ——— PROTEIN ——— BREAD ——— MILK ——— FLOATING ———	FRUIT ——— VEG ——— FAT ——— PROTEIN ——— BREAD ——— MILK ——— FLOATING ———	FRUIT ——— VEG ——— FAT ——— PROTEIN ——— BREAD ——— MILK ——— FLOATING ———	FRUIT ——— VEG ——— FAT ——— PROTEIN ——— BREAD ——— MILK ——— FLOATING ———	FRUIT ——— VEG ——— FAT ——— PROTEIN ——— BREAD ——— MILK ——— FLOATING ———	FRUIT ——— VEG ——— FAT ——— PROTEIN ——— BREAD ——— MILK ——— FLOATING ———
B R E A K F A S T							
L U N C H							
D I N N E R							
S N A C K S							

WEEKLY LIMITS   EGGS ———   CHEESE ———   MEAT ———   ORGAN MEAT ———   OPTIONAL CALORIES ———

I will attend my Weight Watchers meeting this week on ———

MONDAY
20

TUESDAY
21

WEDNESDAY
22

THURSDAY
23

FRIDAY
24

SATURDAY
25

SUNDAY
26

	S	M	T	W	T	F	S
JULY	1	2	3	4	5	6	7
	8	9	10	11	12	13	14
	15	16	17	18	19	20	21
	22	23	24	25	26	27	28
	29	30	31				

	S	M	T	W	T	F	S
				1	2	3	4
AUG	5	6	7	8	9	10	11
	12	13	14	15	16	17	18
	19	20	21	22	23	24	25
	26	27	28	29	30	31	

	S	M	T	W	T	F	S
SEPT							1
	2	3	4	5	6	7	8
	9	10	11	12	13	14	15
	16	17	18	19	20	21	22
	23	24	25	26	27	28	29
	30						

WEEKLY FOOD DIARY

	MONDAY	TUESDAY	WEDNESDAY	THURSDAY	FRIDAY	SATURDAY	SUNDAY
DAILY TOTALS	FRUIT ___ VEG ___ FAT ___ PROTEIN ___ BREAD ___ MILK ___ FLOATING ___		FRUIT ___ VEG ___ FAT ___ PROTEIN ___ BREAD ___ MILK ___ FLOATING ___	FRUIT ___ VEG ___ FAT ___ PROTEIN ___ BREAD ___ MILK ___ FLOATING ___	FRUIT ___ VEG ___ FAT ___ PROTEIN ___ BREAD ___ MILK ___ FLOATING ___	FRUIT ___ VEG ___ FAT ___ PROTEIN ___ BREAD ___ MILK ___ FLOATING ___	FRUIT ___ VEG ___ FAT ___ PROTEIN ___ BREAD ___ MILK ___ FLOATING ___
BREAKFAST							
LUNCH							
DINNER							
SNACKS							

WEEKLY LIMITS   EGGS ___   CHEESE ___   MEAT ___   ORGAN MEAT ___   OPTIONAL CALORIES ___

I will attend my Weight Watchers meeting this week on : ___

ENGAGEMENTS

AUGUST
SEPTEMBER

1 9 9 0

MONDAY
27

TUESDAY
28

WEDNESDAY
29

THURSDAY
30

FRIDAY
31

SATURDAY
1

SUNDAY
2

	S	M	T	W	T	F	S
JULY	1	2	3	4	5	6	7
	8	9	10	11	12	13	14
	15	16	17	18	19	20	21
	22	23	24	25	26	27	28
	29	30	31				

	S	M	T	W	T	F	S
AUG				1	2	3	4
	5	6	7	8	9	10	11
	12	13	14	15	16	17	18
	19	20	21	22	23	24	25
	26	27	28	29	30	31	

	S	M	T	W	T	F	S
SEPT							1
	2	3	4	5	6	7	8
	9	10	11	12	13	14	15
	16	17	18	19	20	21	22
	23	24	25	26	27	28	29
	30						

WEIGHT
RECIPE
WATCHERS

Clams in Tomato-Wine Sauce

Makes 2 servings

2 dozen littleneck clams*
2 tablespoons minced onion
1 tablespoon *each* **chopped fresh**
parsley and basil *or* **1 teaspoon basil**
leaves

2 teaspoons olive *or* **vegetable oil**
2 garlic cloves, minced
¼ cup *each* **canned crushed tomatoes**
and dry white table wine
Dash *each* **salt and pepper**

Microwave Method: Using metal brush, scrub clams and rinse under running cold water. Transfer to large bowl; add cold water to cover and let stand for 10 minutes.

In 1-quart microwavable shallow casserole combine onion, parsley, basil, oil, and garlic; stir well to thoroughly combine. Microwave on High (100%) for 1 minute until onion softens. Add tomatoes and wine and stir to combine. Drain clams and arrange on vegetables; cover with vented plastic wrap and microwave on High for 5 minutes, rotating casserole ½ turn halfway through cooking, until clam shells open. Sprinkle with salt and pepper.

Conventional Method: Using metal brush, scrub clams and rinse under running cold water. Transfer to large bowl; add cold water to cover and let stand for 10 minutes.

In 10-inch nonstick skillet heat oil over high heat; add onion and garlic and sauté until onion softens, 1 to 2 minutes. Add remaining ingredients except clams; stir to combine and cook over high heat until mixture begins to simmer. Drain clams and arrange on vegetables. Reduce heat to medium-low, cover, and cook until clam shells open, 5 to 6 minutes.

Each serving provides: 2 Protein Exchanges; ¼ Vegetable Exchange; 1 Fat Exchange; 30 Optional Calories

Per serving: 139 calories; 12 g protein; 5 g fat; 6 g carbohydrate; 77 mg calcium; 166 mg sodium; 29 mg cholesterol; 0.4 g dietary fiber

* Two dozen littleneck clams will yield about ¼ pound cooked seafood.

Chicken BBQ Style

Makes 2 servings

1 cup diced red onions
¼ cup tomato sauce
1 tablespoon *each* Worcestershire sauce, red wine vinegar, and molasses
2 teaspoons *each* firmly packed brown sugar and Dijon-style mustard

1 teaspoon *each* cornstarch and lemon juice
1 small garlic clove, sliced
1 bay leaf
Dash pepper
2 chicken cutlets (¼ pound each)

Microwave Method: In small microwavable mixing bowl combine all ingredients except chicken, stirring to dissolve cornstarch. Microwave on High (100%) for 5 minutes, stirring once after 2 minutes. Remove and discard bay leaf. Transfer mixture to blender container and process on low speed until pureed.

In 8 × 8 × 2-inch microwavable baking dish arrange chicken; top with onion mixture. Microwave on High for 3 minutes. Turn chicken over and rearrange in dish, moving the portion which has been in the center to the edge. Cover with wax paper and microwave 3 minutes longer. Let stand 1 minute.

Conventional Method: In 1-quart saucepan combine all ingredients except chicken, stirring to dissolve cornstarch. Cook over high heat, stirring constantly, until mixture comes to a boil. Reduce heat to low and let simmer, stirring occasionally, until mixture thickens slightly, about 1 minute. Remove and discard bay leaf. Transfer mixture to blender container and process on low speed until pureed.

Arrange chicken on grill (or baking sheet); brush with half of the onion mixture and cook over hot coals (or in broiler), about 5 minutes. Turn chicken over; brush with remaining onion mixture and cook until chicken is cooked throughout, about 5 minutes longer.

Each serving provides: 3 Protein Exchanges; 1¼ Vegetable Exchanges; 55 Optional Calories
Per serving: 227 calories; 28 g protein; 2 g fat; 24 g carbohydrate; 64 mg calcium; 496 mg sodium; 66 mg cholesterol; 1 g dietary fiber

AUGUST, 1990

WEIGHT
RECIPE
WATCHERS

Eggplant Lasagna

Makes 2 servings

1 medium eggplant (about 1 pound),
   pared and cut lengthwise into ¼-inch-
   thick slices
¾ cup part-skim ricotta cheese
2 ounces mozzarella cheese, shredded
2 tablespoons grated Parmesan cheese
1 tablespoon chopped Italian (flat-leaf)
   parsley

¼ teaspoon oregano leaves
1 cup tomato sauce
3 ounces uncooked curly-edge lasagna
   noodles, cooked according to
   package directions, drained, and cut
   crosswise into halves

Microwave Method: Line microwavable plate with 3 paper towels; arrange half of eggplant in a single layer. Cover with paper towel; microwave on High (100%) for 4 minutes, turning slices over halfway through cooking. Repeat procedure.

In small mixing bowl combine remaining ingredients except sauce and noodles. In 8 × 8 × 2-inch microwavable baking dish spread ¼ cup sauce over noodles; top with half of eggplant. Spread cheese mixture over eggplant; top with remaining eggplant, ¼ cup sauce, remaining noodles and sauce. Cover with vented plastic wrap and microwave on High for 6 minutes, rotating dish ½ turn halfway through cooking. Let stand for 2 minutes.

Conventional Method: Spray 12-inch skillet with nonstick cooking spray; cook half of eggplant over medium-high heat, until softened, 2 to 3 minutes on each side. Transfer to plate; repeat procedure.

Preheat oven to 350°F. In small mixing bowl combine remaining ingredients except sauce and noodles. In 8 × 8 × 2-inch baking dish, layer ingredients as directed in microwave method. Bake uncovered until heated through, about 35 minutes. Let stand for 5 minutes.

Each serving provides: 2½ Protein Exchanges; 4 Vegetable Exchanges; 2 Bread Exchanges; 30 Optional Calories

Per serving: 472 calories; 27 g protein; 16 g fat; 58 g carbohydrate; 566 mg calcium; 1,061 mg sodium; 55 mg cholesterol; 5 g dietary fiber

Lemon Fruit Sauce

Makes 4 servings

¼ cup water
2 tablespoons granulated sugar
1 teaspoon cornstarch

2 teaspoons *each* margarine and
freshly squeezed lemon juice

Microwave Method: In 1-cup microwavable liquid measure combine water, sugar, and cornstarch, stirring to dissolve cornstarch. Microwave on High (100%) for 2 to 2½ minutes, until mixture thickens slightly, stirring once after 1 minute. Using a wire whisk, add margarine, 1 teaspoon at a time, stirring constantly, until margarine is melted and mixture is thoroughly combined. Stir in lemon juice. Let sauce cool slightly and serve warm or cover and refrigerate until chilled, at least 1 hour.

Conventional Method: In small saucepan combine water, sugar, and cornstarch, stirring to dissolve cornstarch. Cook over medium-high heat, stirring constantly, until mixture comes to a boil. Reduce heat and let simmer, stirring constantly, until mixture thickens slightly, about 1 minute; remove from heat. Using a wire whisk, add margarine, 1 teaspoon at a time, stirring constantly, until margarine is melted and mixture is thoroughly combined. Stir in lemon juice. Let sauce cool slightly and serve warm or transfer to bowl, cover, and refrigerate until chilled, at least 1 hour.

Each serving provides: ½ Fat Exchange; 35 Optional Calories

Per serving: 44 calories; trace protein; 2 g fat; 7 g carbohydrate; 0.1 mg calcium; 22 mg sodium; 0 mg cholesterol; dietary fiber data not available

SEPTEMBER

SUNDAY	MONDAY	TUESDAY	WEDNESDAY
2	3	4	5
9	10	11	12
16	17	18	19
23 / 30	24	25	26

SEPTEMBER

THURSDAY	FRIDAY	SATURDAY
		1
6	7	8
13	14	15
20	21	22
27	28	29

Microwave Menu of the Month

Split Pea Soup

Sliced Baked Chicken

Cooked Cauliflower Florets

Arugula, Bibb Lettuce, and Endive Salad with Balsamic Vinegar

Reduced-Calorie Butterscotch Pudding with Oatmeal-Raisin Cookie

Coffee or Tea

NOTES/GOALS

WEEKLY FOOD DIARY

	MONDAY	TUESDAY	WEDNESDAY	THURSDAY	FRIDAY	SATURDAY	SUNDAY
DAILY TOTALS	FRUIT ____ VEG ____ FAT ____ PROTEIN ____ BREAD ____ MILK ____ FLOATING ____	FRUIT ____ VEG ____ FAT ____ PROTEIN ____ BREAD ____ MILK ____ FLOATING ____	FRUIT ____ VEG ____ FAT ____ PROTEIN ____ BREAD ____ MILK ____ FLOATING ____	FRUIT ____ VEG ____ FAT ____ PROTEIN ____ BREAD ____ MILK ____ FLOATING ____	FRUIT ____ VEG ____ FAT ____ PROTEIN ____ BREAD ____ MILK ____ FLOATING ____	FRUIT ____ VEG ____ FAT ____ PROTEIN ____ BREAD ____ MILK ____ FLOATING ____	FRUIT ____ VEG ____ FAT ____ PROTEIN ____ BREAD ____ MILK ____ FLOATING ____
BREAKFAST							
LUNCH							
DINNER							
SNACKS							

WEEKLY LIMITS   EGGS ____   CHEESE ____   MEAT ____   ORGAN MEAT ____   OPTIONAL CALORIES ____

I will attend my Weight Watchers meeting this week on _____

ENGAGEMENTS

SEPTEMBER

1990

Labor Day

MONDAY
3

TUESDAY
4

WEDNESDAY
5

THURSDAY
6

FRIDAY
7

SATURDAY
8

SUNDAY
9

	S	M	T	W	T	F	S
				1	2	3	4
A	5	6	7	8	9	10	11
U	12	13	14	15	16	17	18
G	19	20	21	22	23	24	25
	26	27	28	29	30	31	

	S	M	T	W	T	F	S
							1
S	2	3	4	5	6	7	8
E	9	10	11	12	13	14	15
P	16	17	18	19	20	21	22
T	23	24	25	26	27	28	29
	30						

	S	M	T	W	T	F	S
		1	2	3	4	5	6
O	7	8	9	10	11	12	13
C	14	15	16	17	18	19	20
T	21	22	23	24	25	26	27
	28	29	30	31			

WEEKLY FOOD DIARY

	MONDAY	TUESDAY	WEDNESDAY	THURSDAY	FRIDAY	SATURDAY	SUNDAY
DAILY TOTALS	FRUIT ___ VEG ___ FAT ___ PROTEIN ___ BREAD ___ MILK ___ FLOATING ___	FRUIT ___ VEG ___ FAT ___ PROTEIN ___ BREAD ___ MILK ___ FLOATING ___	FRUIT ___ VEG ___ FAT ___ PROTEIN ___ BREAD ___ MILK ___ FLOATING ___	FRUIT ___ VEG ___ FAT ___ PROTEIN ___ BREAD ___ MILK ___ FLOATING ___	FRUIT ___ VEG ___ FAT ___ PROTEIN ___ BREAD ___ MILK ___ FLOATING ___	FRUIT ___ VEG ___ FAT ___ PROTEIN ___ BREAD ___ MILK ___ FLOATING ___	FRUIT ___ VEG ___ FAT ___ PROTEIN ___ BREAD ___ MILK ___ FLOATING ___
BREAKFAST							
LUNCH							
DINNER							
SNACKS							

WEEKLY LIMITS EGGS ___ CHEESE ___ MEAT ___ ORGAN MEAT ___ OPTIONAL CALORIES ___

I will attend my Weight Watchers meeting this week on _____

MONDAY
10

TUESDAY
11

WEDNESDAY
12

THURSDAY
13

FRIDAY
14

SATURDAY
15

SUNDAY
16

	S	M	T	W	T	F	S
				1	2	3	4
A	5	6	7	8	9	10	11
U	12	13	14	15	16	17	18
G	19	20	21	22	23	24	25
	26	27	28	29	30	31	

	S	M	T	W	T	F	S
							1
S	2	3	4	5	6	7	8
E	9	10	11	12	13	14	15
P	16	17	18	19	20	21	22
T	23	24	25	26	27	28	29
	30						

	S	M	T	W	T	F	S
		1	2	3	4	5	6
O	7	8	9	10	11	12	13
C	14	15	16	17	18	19	20
T	21	22	23	24	25	26	27
	28	29	30	31			

WEEKLY FOOD DIARY

	MONDAY	TUESDAY	WEDNESDAY	THURSDAY	FRIDAY	SATURDAY	SUNDAY
DAILY TOTALS	FRUIT ____ VEG ____ FAT ____ PROTEIN ____ BREAD ____ MILK ____ FLOATING ____	FRUIT ____ VEG ____ FAT ____ PROTEIN ____ BREAD ____ MILK ____ FLOATING ____	FRUIT ____ VEG ____ FAT ____ PROTEIN ____ BREAD ____ MILK ____ FLOATING ____	FRUIT ____ VEG ____ FAT ____ PROTEIN ____ BREAD ____ MILK ____ FLOATING ____	FRUIT ____ VEG ____ FAT ____ PROTEIN ____ BREAD ____ MILK ____ FLOATING ____	FRUIT ____ VEG ____ FAT ____ PROTEIN ____ BREAD ____ MILK ____ FLOATING ____	FRUIT ____ VEG ____ FAT ____ PROTEIN ____ BREAD ____ MILK ____ FLOATING ____
BREAKFAST							
LUNCH							
DINNER							
SNACKS							

WEEKLY LIMITS EGGS ____ CHEESE ____ MEAT ____ ORGAN MEAT ____ OPTIONAL CALORIES ____

I will attend my Weight Watchers meeting this week on ____

MONDAY
17

TUESDAY
18

WEDNESDAY
19

First Day of Rosh Hashanah

THURSDAY
20

FRIDAY
21

SATURDAY
22

SUNDAY
23

	S	M	T	W	T	F	S
				1	2	3	4
A	5	6	7	8	9	10	11
U	12	13	14	15	16	17	18
G	19	20	21	22	23	24	25
	26	27	28	29	30	31	

	S	M	T	W	T	F	S
							1
S	2	3	4	5	6	7	8
E	9	10	11	12	13	14	15
P	16	17	18	19	20	21	22
T	23	24	25	26	27	28	29
	30						

	S	M	T	W	T	F	S
		1	2	3	4	5	6
O	7	8	9	10	11	12	13
C	14	15	16	17	18	19	20
T	21	22	23	24	25	26	27
	28	29	30	31			

WEEKLY FOOD DIARY

	MONDAY	TUESDAY	WEDNESDAY	THURSDAY	FRIDAY	SATURDAY	SUNDAY
DAILY TOTALS	FRUIT ___ VEG ___ FAT ___ PROTEIN ___ BREAD ___ MILK ___ FLOATING ___	FRUIT ___ VEG ___ FAT ___ PROTEIN ___ BREAD ___ MILK ___ FLOATING ___	FRUIT ___ VEG ___ FAT ___ PROTEIN ___ BREAD ___ MILK ___ FLOATING ___	FRUIT ___ VEG ___ FAT ___ PROTEIN ___ BREAD ___ MILK ___ FLOATING ___	FRUIT ___ VEG ___ FAT ___ PROTEIN ___ BREAD ___ MILK ___ FLOATING ___	FRUIT ___ VEG ___ FAT ___ PROTEIN ___ BREAD ___ MILK ___ FLOATING ___	FRUIT ___ VEG ___ FAT ___ PROTEIN ___ BREAD ___ MILK ___ FLOATING ___
BREAKFAST							
LUNCH							
DINNER							
SNACKS							

WEEKLY LIMITS   EGGS ___   CHEESE ___   MEAT ___   ORGAN MEAT ___   OPTIONAL CALORIES ___

I will attend my Weight Watchers meeting this week on _____

ENGAGEMENTS

SEPTEMBER

1 9 9 0

MONDAY
24

TUESDAY
25

WEDNESDAY
26

THURSDAY
27

FRIDAY
28

Yom Kippur

SATURDAY
29

SUNDAY
30

	S	M	T	W	T	F	S
				1	2	3	4
A	5	6	7	8	9	10	11
U	12	13	14	15	16	17	18
G	19	20	21	22	23	24	25
	26	27	28	29	30	31	

	S	M	T	W	T	F	S
							1
S	2	3	4	5	6	7	8
E	9	10	11	12	13	14	15
P	16	17	18	19	20	21	22
T	23	24	25	26	27	28	29
	30						

	S	M	T	W	T	F	S
		1	2	3	4	5	6
O	7	8	9	10	11	12	13
C	14	15	16	17	18	19	20
T	21	22	23	24	25	26	27
	28	29	30	31			

WEIGHT
RECIPE
WATCHERS

Split Pea Soup

Makes 2 servings, about 1 cup each

½ cup diced onion
2 teaspoons olive *or* vegetable oil
1 garlic clove, minced
3 cups water
2¼ ounces uncooked green split peas,
   rinsed and sorted

1 bay leaf
Dash marjoram leaves
½ cup *each* diced carrot and celery
¼ pound frankfurters, sliced

Microwave Method: In 1-quart microwavable casserole combine onion, oil, and garlic; stir well to thoroughly combine. Microwave on High (100%) for 1 minute. Add water, peas, and seasonings and stir to combine. Cover tightly with plastic wrap and microwave on High for 5 minutes. Using a knife, pierce plastic wrap in several places to release steam; remove plastic wrap. Add carrot and celery and stir to combine; cover tightly with new sheet of plastic wrap and microwave on High for 20 to 25 minutes until peas are tender, stirring twice during cooking. Pierce plastic wrap and remove; add frankfurters and stir to combine. Cover with vented plastic wrap and microwave on High until heated through and peas are very soft, about 5 minutes longer. Remove and discard bay leaf.

Conventional Method: In 1-quart saucepan heat oil; add onion and garlic and sauté over medium heat until onion is translucent, about 2 minutes. Add water, peas, and seasonings and stir to combine. Cook over medium heat until mixture comes to a boil. Add carrot and celery and stir to combine; return to a boil. Reduce heat to low, cover, and let simmer, stirring occasionally, until peas are tender, about 40 minutes. Add frankfurters and stir to combine; cover and cook until heated through and peas are very soft, about 5 minutes longer. Remove and discard bay leaf.

Each serving provides: 2 Protein Exchanges; 1½ Bread Exchanges; 1½ Vegetable Exchanges; 1 Fat Exchange

Per serving: 368 calories; 15 g protein; 22 g fat; 29 g carbohydrate; 61 mg calcium; 680 mg sodium; 28 mg cholesterol; 3 g dietary fiber

Macaroni and Cheese

Makes 2 servings

½ cup skim *or* nonfat milk
¼ cup evaporated skimmed milk
1 tablespoon *each* minced onion and
   cornstarch
1 teaspoon Dijon-style mustard

⅛ teaspoon *each* salt and pepper
3 ounces Cheddar cheese, shredded,
   divided
1½ cups cooked elbow macaroni

Microwave Method: In 1-quart microwavable casserole combine all ingredients except cheese and macaroni, stirring well to combine. Cover with vented plastic wrap; microwave on High (100%) for 2 minutes. Stir in 1½ ounces cheese; cover with vented plastic wrap and microwave on High for 30 seconds. Stir in macaroni; replace vented plastic wrap and microwave on High for 2 minutes. Sprinkle with remaining 1½ ounces cheese and microwave on High, uncovered, for 30 seconds until cheese melts.

Conventional Method: Preheat oven to 350°F. In 1½-quart saucepan combine all ingredients except cheese and macaroni, stirring well to combine. Cook over medium heat until mixture just begins to simmer, about 2 minutes. Add 1½ ounces cheese and stir to combine; continuing to stir, cook until cheese is melted and mixture thickens, about 1 minute. Stir in macaroni.

Spray 1-quart casserole with nonstick cooking spray; transfer macaroni mixture to casserole and sprinkle with remaining 1½ ounces cheese. Bake until cheese is melted and lightly browned, about 20 minutes.

Each serving provides: 1½ Protein Exchanges; 1½ Bread Exchanges; ½ Milk Exchange; 15 Optional Calories

Per serving: 354 calories; 19 g protein; 15 g fat; 36 g carbohydrate; 486 mg calcium; 547 mg sodium; 47 mg cholesterol; 1 g dietary fiber

WEIGHT RECIPE WATCHERS

Stuffed Baked Potato

Makes 2 servings

2 baked potatoes (3 ounces each)
2 teaspoons margarine
½ cup broccoli florets, blanched
¼ cup sliced mushrooms

2 slices crisp bacon, crumbled
1 tablespoon sliced scallion (green onion)
1 ounce Cheddar cheese, shredded

Microwave Method: Cut a thin lengthwise slice from each potato and, using a spoon, scoop out pulp from each slice and discard peel. Scoop out pulp from each potato, leaving two ¼-inch-thick shells. In small mixing bowl combine potato pulp and margarine and mash. Spoon half of potato mixture into each reserved shell. Top each potato with half of the broccoli, mushrooms, bacon, and scallion; then top each with ½ ounce of cheese. Set stuffed potatoes on microwavable plate and microwave on High (100%) for 1 minute until potatoes are thoroughly heated and cheese is melted.

Conventional Method: Cut a thin lengthwise slice from each potato and, using a spoon, scoop out pulp from each slice and discard peel. Scoop out pulp from each potato, leaving two ¼-inch-thick shells. In small mixing bowl combine potato pulp and margarine and mash. Spoon half of potato mixture into each reserved shell. Top each potato with half of the broccoli, mushrooms, bacon, and scallion; then top each with ½ ounce of cheese. Set stuffed potatoes on nonstick baking sheet and broil until potatoes are thoroughly heated and cheese is melted, about 2 minutes.

Each serving provides: ½ Protein Exchange; 1 Bread Exchange; ¾ Vegetable Exchange; 1 Fat Exchange; 45 Optional Calories

Per serving: 233 calories; 9 g protein; 12 g fat; 24 g carbohydrate; 129 mg calcium; 249 mg sodium; 20 mg cholesterol; 2 g dietary fiber

Marshmallow Clusters

Makes 2 servings, 2 clusters each

1 ounce semisweet chocolate chips
¼ ounce miniature marshmallows

1 graham cracker (2½-inch square),
broken into small pieces

Microwave Method: In small microwavable bowl microwave chocolate on High (100%) for 45 seconds until chocolate is melted. Stir in marshmallows and graham cracker pieces.

Spray nonstick cookie sheet with nonstick cooking spray. Spoon chocolate mixture onto cookie sheet, making 4 equal mounds. Cover and refrigerate until chocolate hardens, about 30 minutes.

Conventional Method: Fill bottom half of double boiler halfway with water and bring to a boil; remove from heat. Add chocolate to top half of double boiler and set over boiling water; let stand until chocolate melts, about 3 minutes.* Stir in marshmallows and graham cracker pieces.

Spray nonstick cookie sheet with nonstick cooking spray. Spoon chocolate mixture onto cookie sheet, making 4 equal mounds. Cover and refrigerate until chocolate hardens, about 30 minutes.

Each serving provides: ¼ Bread Exchange; 90 Optional Calories

Per serving: 97 calories; 1 g protein; 5 g fat; 14 g carbohydrate; 6 mg calcium; 25 mg sodium; trace cholesterol; 0.4 g dietary fiber

* When melting chocolate, it should not come in contact with water or steam; moisture will cause it to harden.

OCTOBER

SUNDAY	MONDAY	TUESDAY	WEDNESDAY
	1	2	3
7	8	9	10
14	15	16	17
21	22	23	24
28	29	30	31

OCTOBER

THURSDAY	FRIDAY	SATURDAY
4	5	6
11	12	13
18	19	20
25	26	27

Microwave Menu of the Month

Ham and Swiss Cheese with Dijon-Style Mustard on Pumpernickel Bread

Tomato and Zucchini Slices on Lettuce leaves

Peanut Brittle

Unfermented Apple Cider

NOTES/GOALS

WEEKLY FOOD DIARY

	MONDAY	TUESDAY	WEDNESDAY	THURSDAY	FRIDAY	SATURDAY	SUNDAY
DAILY TOTALS	FRUIT _____ VEG _____ FAT _____ PROTEIN _____ BREAD _____ MILK _____ FLOATING _____	FRUIT _____ VEG _____ FAT _____ PROTEIN _____ BREAD _____ MILK _____ FLOATING _____	FRUIT _____ VEG _____ FAT _____ PROTEIN _____ BREAD _____ MILK _____ FLOATING _____	FRUIT _____ VEG _____ FAT _____ PROTEIN _____ BREAD _____ MILK _____ FLOATING _____	FRUIT _____ VEG _____ FAT _____ PROTEIN _____ BREAD _____ MILK _____ FLOATING _____	FRUIT _____ VEG _____ FAT _____ PROTEIN _____ BREAD _____ MILK _____ FLOATING _____	FRUIT _____ VEG _____ FAT _____ PROTEIN _____ BREAD _____ MILK _____ FLOATING _____
BREAKFAST							
LUNCH							
DINNER							
SNACKS							

WEEKLY LIMITS EGGS _____   CHEESE _____   MEAT _____   ORGAN MEAT _____   OPTIONAL CALORIES _____

I will attend my Weight Watchers meeting this week on _____

ENGAGEMENTS

OCTOBER

1 9 9 0

MONDAY
1

TUESDAY
2

WEDNESDAY
3

THURSDAY
4

FRIDAY
5

SATURDAY
6

SUNDAY
7

	S	M	T	W	T	F	S
							1
S	2	3	4	5	6	7	8
E	9	10	11	12	13	14	15
P	16	17	18	19	20	21	22
T	23	24	25	26	27	28	29
	30						

	S	M	T	W	T	F	S
		1	2	3	4	5	6
O	7	8	9	10	11	12	13
C	14	15	16	17	18	19	20
T	21	22	23	24	25	26	27
	28	29	30	31			

	S	M	T	W	T	F	S
					1	2	3
N	4	5	6	7	8	9	10
O	11	12	13	14	15	16	17
V	18	19	20	21	22	23	24
	25	26	27	28	29	30	

WEEKLY FOOD DIARY

	MONDAY	TUESDAY	WEDNESDAY	THURSDAY	FRIDAY	SATURDAY	SUNDAY
DAILY TOTALS	FRUIT ___ VEG ___ FAT ___ PROTEIN ___ BREAD ___ MILK ___ FLOATING ___	FRUIT ___ VEG ___ FAT ___ PROTEIN ___ BREAD ___ MILK ___ FLOATING ___	FRUIT ___ VEG ___ FAT ___ PROTEIN ___ BREAD ___ MILK ___ FLOATING ___	FRUIT ___ VEG ___ FAT ___ PROTEIN ___ BREAD ___ MILK ___ FLOATING ___	FRUIT ___ VEG ___ FAT ___ PROTEIN ___ BREAD ___ MILK ___ FLOATING ___	FRUIT ___ VEG ___ FAT ___ PROTEIN ___ BREAD ___ MILK ___ FLOATING ___	FRUIT ___ VEG ___ FAT ___ PROTEIN ___ BREAD ___ MILK ___ FLOATING ___
BREAKFAST							
LUNCH							
DINNER							
SNACKS							

WEEKLY LIMITS   EGGS ___   CHEESE ___   MEAT ___   ORGAN MEAT ___   OPTIONAL CALORIES ___

I will attend my Weight Watchers meeting this week on ___

ENGAGEMENTS

OCTOBER

1990

Columbus Day (observed)
Thanksgiving Day (Canada)

MONDAY
8

TUESDAY
9

WEDNESDAY
10

THURSDAY
11

Columbus Day

FRIDAY
12

SATURDAY
13

SUNDAY
14

	S	M	T	W	T	F	S
							1
S	2	3	4	5	6	7	8
E	9	10	11	12	13	14	15
P	16	17	18	19	20	21	22
T	23	24	25	26	27	28	29
	30						

	S	M	T	W	T	F	S
		1	2	3	4	5	6
O	7	8	9	10	11	12	13
C	14	15	16	17	18	19	20
T	21	22	23	24	25	26	27
	28	29	30	31			

	S	M	T	W	T	F	S
					1	2	3
N	4	5	6	7	8	9	10
O	11	12	13	14	15	16	17
V	18	19	20	21	22	23	24
	25	26	27	28	29	30	

WEEKLY FOOD DIARY

	MONDAY	TUESDAY	WEDNESDAY	THURSDAY	FRIDAY	SATURDAY	SUNDAY
DAILY TOTALS	FRUIT ___ VEG ___ FAT ___ PROTEIN ___ BREAD ___ MILK ___ FLOATING ___	FRUIT ___ VEG ___ FAT ___ PROTEIN ___ BREAD ___ MILK ___ FLOATING ___	FRUIT ___ VEG ___ FAT ___ PROTEIN ___ BREAD ___ MILK ___ FLOATING ___	FRUIT ___ VEG ___ FAT ___ PROTEIN ___ BREAD ___ MILK ___ FLOATING ___	FRUIT ___ VEG ___ FAT ___ PROTEIN ___ BREAD ___ MILK ___ FLOATING ___	FRUIT ___ VEG ___ FAT ___ PROTEIN ___ BREAD ___ MILK ___ FLOATING ___	FRUIT ___ VEG ___ FAT ___ PROTEIN ___ BREAD ___ MILK ___ FLOATING ___
BREAKFAST							
LUNCH							
DINNER							
SNACKS							

WEEKLY LIMITS EGGS ___ CHEESE ___ MEAT ___ ORGAN MEAT ___ OPTIONAL CALORIES ___

I will attend my Weight Watchers meeting this week on ___

MONDAY
15

TUESDAY
16

WEDNESDAY
17

THURSDAY
18

FRIDAY
19

SATURDAY
20

SUNDAY
21

	S	M	T	W	T	F	S
S							1
E	2	3	4	5	6	7	8
P	9	10	11	12	13	14	15
T	16	17	18	19	20	21	22
	23	24	25	26	27	28	29
	30						

	S	M	T	W	T	F	S
		1	2	3	4	5	6
O	7	8	9	10	11	12	13
C	14	15	16	17	18	19	20
T	21	22	23	24	25	26	27
	28	29	30	31			

	S	M	T	W	T	F	S
					1	2	3
N	4	5	6	7	8	9	10
O	11	12	13	14	15	16	17
V	18	19	20	21	22	23	24
	25	26	27	28	29	30	

WEEKLY FOOD DIARY

	MONDAY	TUESDAY	WEDNESDAY	THURSDAY	FRIDAY	SATURDAY	SUNDAY
DAILY TOTALS	FRUIT ___ VEG ___ FAT ___ PROTEIN ___ BREAD ___ MILK ___ FLOATING ___	FRUIT ___ VEG ___ FAT ___ PROTEIN ___ BREAD ___ MILK ___ FLOATING ___	FRUIT ___ VEG ___ FAT ___ PROTEIN ___ BREAD ___ MILK ___ FLOATING ___	FRUIT ___ VEG ___ FAT ___ PROTEIN ___ BREAD ___ MILK ___ FLOATING ___	FRUIT ___ VEG ___ FAT ___ PROTEIN ___ BREAD ___ MILK ___ FLOATING ___	FRUIT ___ VEG ___ FAT ___ PROTEIN ___ BREAD ___ MILK ___ FLOATING ___	FRUIT ___ VEG ___ FAT ___ PROTEIN ___ BREAD ___ MILK ___ FLOATING ___
BREAKFAST							
LUNCH							
DINNER							
SNACKS							

WEEKLY LIMITS   EGGS _____   CHEESE _____   MEAT _____   ORGAN MEAT _____   OPTIONAL CALORIES _____

I will attend my Weight Watchers meeting this week on _____

ENGAGEMENTS

OCTOBER

1 9 9 0

MONDAY
22

TUESDAY
23

United Nations Day

WEDNESDAY
24

THURSDAY
25

FRIDAY
26

SATURDAY
27

SUNDAY
28

	S	M	T	W	T	F	S
							1
S	2	3	4	5	6	7	8
E	9	10	11	12	13	14	15
P	16	17	18	19	20	21	22
T	23	24	25	26	27	28	29
	30						

	S	M	T	W	T	F	S
		1	2	3	4	5	6
O	7	8	9	10	11	12	13
C	14	15	16	17	18	19	20
T	21	22	23	24	25	26	27
	28	29	30	31			

	S	M	T	W	T	F	S
					1	2	3
N	4	5	6	7	8	9	10
O	11	12	13	14	15	16	17
V	18	19	20	21	22	23	24
	25	26	27	28	29	30	

Spiced Tomato Soup

Makes 2 servings, about 1½ cups each

¼ cup *each* thinly sliced onion, celery, carrot, and green bell pepper
2 teaspoons olive *or* vegetable oil
1 small garlic clove, minced
2 cups tomato juice
2 tablespoons freshly squeezed lemon juice
1 tablespoon prepared horseradish

1 teaspoon Worcestershire sauce
2 to 3 drops hot sauce
1 bay leaf
Dash *each* marjoram leaves, basil leaves, thyme leaves, and pepper
Garnish: 2 *each* celery sticks and lemon wedges

Microwave Method: In 1-quart microwavable casserole combine vegetables, oil, and garlic; stir well to thoroughly combine. Microwave on High (100%) for 4 minutes until vegetables are softened, stirring halfway through cooking. Add remaining ingredients except garnish, stirring to thoroughly combine; microwave on High for 3 minutes until heated through, stirring once halfway through cooking. Remove and discard bay leaf. Divide into two 12-ounce mugs; garnish each portion with 1 celery stick and lemon wedge.

Conventional Method: In 1-quart saucepan heat oil; add vegetables and garlic and cook over medium heat, stirring frequently, until vegetables are softened, about 10 minutes. Add remaining ingredients except garnish, stirring to thoroughly combine; bring mixture to a boil. Reduce heat to low and let simmer until flavors blend, about 10 minutes. Remove and discard bay leaf. Divide into two 12-ounce mugs; garnish each portion with 1 celery stick and lemon wedge.

Each serving provides: 2 Vegetable Exchanges; 1 Fat Exchange

Per serving: 118 calories; 3 g protein; 5 g fat; 20 g carbohydrate; 63 mg calcium; 946 mg sodium; 0 mg cholesterol; 1 g dietary fiber (this figure does not include tomato juice; nutrition analysis not available)

Stuffed Pepper

Makes 1 serving

1 large green bell pepper (about 7 ounces)
3 ounces ground veal
¼ cup *each* diced onion, celery, and mushrooms
½ teaspoon vegetable oil
1 garlic clove, minced

½ cup cooked instant rice
¼ cup tomato sauce
Dash *each* salt, pepper, and thyme leaves
1 teaspoon chopped Italian (flat-leaf) parsley

Microwave Method: Cut pepper in half lengthwise; remove and discard seeds and membranes. In 8 × 8 × 2-inch microwavable baking pan arrange pepper halves cut-side down. Cover with vented plastic wrap and microwave on High (100%) for 4 minutes until tender, rotating casserole ½ turn halfway through cooking. Transfer pepper to sheet of paper towel; set aside.

In same pan combine veal, vegetables, oil, and garlic; stir well to thoroughly combine. Microwave on High for 2 minutes until veal is no longer pink; add remaining ingredients except parsley and stir to combine. Spoon half of rice mixture into each pepper half; sprinkle with parsley and set halves in same casserole. Microwave pepper on High for 2 minutes until heated through, rotating casserole ½ turn halfway through cooking.

Conventional Method: In small skillet heat oil; add veal, vegetables, and garlic and cook over medium heat until veal is no longer pink, 3 to 4 minutes. Remove from heat; add remaining ingredients except parsley and stir to combine.

Preheat oven to 350°F. Cut pepper in half lengthwise; remove and discard seeds and membranes. Spoon half of rice mixture into each pepper half; sprinkle with parsley. In 8 × 8 × 2-inch nonstick baking pan arrange peppers; cover and bake until heated through, about 20 minutes.

Each serving provides: 2 Protein Exchanges; 1 Bread Exchange; 6 Vegetable Exchanges; ½ Fat Exchange

Per serving: 360 calories; 22 g protein; 13 g fat; 40 g carbohydrate; 63 mg calcium; 608 mg sodium; 64 mg cholesterol; 3 g dietary fiber (this figure does not include instant rice; nutrition analysis not available)

Peanut Brittle

Makes 4 servings

¼ cup granulated sugar
2 tablespoons *each* light corn syrup
and water

1 ounce shelled unsalted roasted
peanuts, chopped

Microwave Method: In small microwavable mixing bowl combine sugar, syrup, and water, stirring to combine. Microwave on High (100%) for 5 minutes until mixture is golden brown; stir in nuts. Spray nonstick cookie sheet with nonstick cooking spray; pour nut mixture onto cookie sheet and let stand until mixture cools slightly, about 2 minutes. Using a rolling pin, roll peanut mixture into a 6-inch square; cut into 4 equal portions. Transfer to wire rack and let stand until completely hardened, 10 to 15 minutes.

Conventional Method: In small saucepan combine sugar, syrup, and water and cook over high heat until sugar is dissolved and mixture comes to a boil. Set candy thermometer in pan and continue boiling until temperature reaches 325°F and mixture is golden brown, 6 to 8 minutes. Remove from heat and stir in nuts. Spray nonstick cookie sheet with nonstick cooking spray; pour nut mixture onto cookie sheet and let stand until mixture cools slightly, about 2 minutes. Using a rolling pin, roll peanut mixture into a 6-inch square; cut into 4 equal portions. Transfer to wire rack and let stand until completely hardened, 10 to 15 minutes.

Each serving provides: ½ Protein Exchange; ½ Fat Exchange; 90 Optional Calories

Per serving: 119 calories; 2 g protein; 3 g fat; 21 g carbohydrate; 11 mg calcium; 8 mg sodium; 0 mg cholesterol; 1 g dietary fiber

THURSDAY	FRIDAY	SATURDAY
1	2	3
8	9	10
15	16	17
22	23	24
29	30	

Microwave Menu of the Month

Roast Turkey

Acorn Squash and Cheddar Gratin

Honey-Glazed Carrot Sticks

Shredded Red Cabbage, Sliced Celery, and Sliced Radishes on Boston Lettuce with French Dressing

Cinnamon-Baked Apple topped with Whipped Cream

White Wine

NOTES/GOALS

WEEKLY FOOD DIARY

	MONDAY	TUESDAY	WEDNESDAY	THURSDAY	FRIDAY	SATURDAY	SUNDAY
DAILY TOTALS	FRUIT ——— VEG ——— FAT ——— PROTEIN ——— BREAD ——— MILK ——— FLOATING ———	FRUIT ——— VEG ——— FAT ——— PROTEIN ——— BREAD ——— MILK ——— FLOATING ———	FRUIT ——— VEG ——— FAT ——— PROTEIN ——— BREAD ——— MILK ——— FLOATING ———	FRUIT ——— VEG ——— FAT ——— PROTEIN ——— BREAD ——— MILK ——— FLOATING ———	FRUIT ——— VEG ——— FAT ——— PROTEIN ——— BREAD ——— MILK ——— FLOATING ———	FRUIT ——— VEG ——— FAT ——— PROTEIN ——— BREAD ——— MILK ——— FLOATING ———	FRUIT ——— VEG ——— FAT ——— PROTEIN ——— BREAD ——— MILK ——— FLOATING ———
BREAKFAST							
LUNCH							
DINNER							
SNACKS							

WEEKLY LIMITS   EGGS ———   CHEESE ———   MEAT ———   ORGAN MEAT ———   OPTIONAL CALORIES ———

I will attend my Weight Watchers meeting this week on ————————

OCTOBER
NOVEMBER

1 9 9 0

MONDAY
29

TUESDAY
30

Halloween

WEDNESDAY
31

THURSDAY
1

FRIDAY
2

SATURDAY
3

SUNDAY
4

	S	M	T	W	T	F	S
		1	2	3	4	5	6
O	7	8	9	10	11	12	13
C	14	15	16	17	18	19	20
T	21	22	23	24	25	26	27
	28	29	30	31			

	S	M	T	W	T	F	S
					1	2	3
N	4	5	6	7	8	9	10
O	11	12	13	14	15	16	17
V	18	19	20	21	22	23	24
	25	26	27	28	29	30	

	S	M	T	W	T	F	S
							1
D	2	3	4	5	6	7	8
E	9	10	11	12	13	14	15
C	16	17	18	19	20	21	22
	23	24	25	26	27	28	29
	30	31					

WEEKLY FOOD DIARY

	MONDAY	TUESDAY	WEDNESDAY	THURSDAY	FRIDAY	SATURDAY	SUNDAY
DAILY TOTALS	FRUIT ___ VEG ___ FAT ___ PROTEIN ___ BREAD ___ MILK ___ FLOATING ___	FRUIT ___ VEG ___ FAT ___ PROTEIN ___ BREAD ___ MILK ___ FLOATING ___	FRUIT ___ VEG ___ FAT ___ PROTEIN ___ BREAD ___ MILK ___ FLOATING ___	FRUIT ___ VEG ___ FAT ___ PROTEIN ___ BREAD ___ MILK ___ FLOATING ___	FRUIT ___ VEG ___ FAT ___ PROTEIN ___ BREAD ___ MILK ___ FLOATING ___	FRUIT ___ VEG ___ FAT ___ PROTEIN ___ BREAD ___ MILK ___ FLOATING ___	FRUIT ___ VEG ___ FAT ___ PROTEIN ___ BREAD ___ MILK ___ FLOATING ___
BREAKFAST							
LUNCH							
DINNER							
SNACKS							

WEEKLY LIMITS   EGGS _____   CHEESE _____   MEAT _____   ORGAN MEAT _____   OPTIONAL CALORIES _____

I will attend my Weight Watchers meeting this week on _____

MONDAY
5

Election Day

TUESDAY
6

WEDNESDAY
7

THURSDAY
8

FRIDAY
9

SATURDAY
10

Veterans Day
Armistice Day (Canada)

SUNDAY
11

	S	M	T	W	T	F	S
		1	2	3	4	5	6
O	7	8	9	10	11	12	13
C	14	15	16	17	18	19	20
T	21	22	23	24	25	26	27
	28	29	30	31			

	S	M	T	W	T	F	S
					1	2	3
N	4	5	6	7	8	9	10
O	11	12	13	14	15	16	17
V	18	19	20	21	22	23	24
	25	26	27	28	29	30	

	S	M	T	W	T	F	S
							1
D	2	3	4	5	6	7	8
E	9	10	11	12	13	14	15
C	16	17	18	19	20	21	22
	23	24	25	26	27	28	29
	30	31					

WEEKLY FOOD DIARY

	MONDAY	TUESDAY	WEDNESDAY	THURSDAY	FRIDAY	SATURDAY	SUNDAY
D A I L Y T O T A L S	FRUIT _____ VEG _____ FAT _____ PROTEIN _____ BREAD _____ MILK _____ FLOATING _____	FRUIT _____ VEG _____ FAT _____ PROTEIN _____ BREAD _____ MILK _____ FLOATING _____	FRUIT _____ VEG _____ FAT _____ PROTEIN _____ BREAD _____ MILK _____ FLOATING _____	FRUIT _____ VEG _____ FAT _____ PROTEIN _____ BREAD _____ MILK _____ FLOATING _____	FRUIT _____ VEG _____ FAT _____ PROTEIN _____ BREAD _____ MILK _____ FLOATING _____	FRUIT _____ VEG _____ FAT _____ PROTEIN _____ BREAD _____ MILK _____ FLOATING _____	FRUIT _____ VEG _____ FAT _____ PROTEIN _____ BREAD _____ MILK _____ FLOATING _____
B R E A K F A S T							
L U N C H							
D I N N E R							
S N A C K S							

WEEKLY LIMITS EGGS _____   CHEESE _____   MEAT _____   ORGAN MEAT _____   OPTIONAL CALORIES _____

I will attend my Weight Watchers meeting this week on _____

NOVEMBER

1990

MONDAY
12

TUESDAY
13

WEDNESDAY
14

THURSDAY
15

FRIDAY
16

SATURDAY
17

SUNDAY
18

	S	M	T	W	T	F	S
					1	2	3
O	7	8	9	10	11	12	13
C	14	15	16	17	18	19	20
T	21	22	23	24	25	26	27
	28	29	30	31			

	S	M	T	W	T	F	S
					1	2	3
N	4	5	6	7	8	9	10
O	11	12	13	14	15	16	17
V	18	19	20	21	22	23	24
	25	26	27	28	29	30	

	S	M	T	W	T	F	S
							1
D	2	3	4	5	6	7	8
E	9	10	11	12	13	14	15
C	16	17	18	19	20	21	22
	23	24	25	26	27	28	29
	30	31					

WEEKLY FOOD DIARY

	MONDAY	TUESDAY	WEDNESDAY	THURSDAY	FRIDAY	SATURDAY	SUNDAY
DAILY TOTALS	FRUIT ____ VEG ____ FAT ____ PROTEIN ____ BREAD ____ MILK ____ FLOATING ____	FRUIT ____ VEG ____ FAT ____ PROTEIN ____ BREAD ____ MILK ____ FLOATING ____	FRUIT ____ VEG ____ FAT ____ PROTEIN ____ BREAD ____ MILK ____ FLOATING ____	FRUIT ____ VEG ____ FAT ____ PROTEIN ____ BREAD ____ MILK ____ FLOATING ____	FRUIT ____ VEG ____ FAT ____ PROTEIN ____ BREAD ____ MILK ____ FLOATING ____	FRUIT ____ VEG ____ FAT ____ PROTEIN ____ BREAD ____ MILK ____ FLOATING ____	FRUIT ____ VEG ____ FAT ____ PROTEIN ____ BREAD ____ MILK ____ FLOATING ____
BREAKFAST							
LUNCH							
DINNER							
SNACKS							

WEEKLY LIMITS EGGS ____ CHEESE ____ MEAT ____ ORGAN MEAT ____ OPTIONAL CALORIES ____

I will attend my Weight Watchers meeting this week on ____

MONDAY
19

TUESDAY
20

WEDNESDAY
21

Thanksgiving Day

THURSDAY
22

FRIDAY
23

SATURDAY
24

SUNDAY
25

	S	M	T	W	T	F	S
		1	2	3	4	5	6
O	7	8	9	10	11	12	13
C	14	15	16	17	18	19	20
T	21	22	23	24	25	26	27
	28	29	30	31			

	S	M	T	W	T	F	S
					1	2	3
N	4	5	6	7	8	9	10
O	11	12	13	14	15	16	17
V	18	19	20	21	22	23	24
	25	26	27	28	29	30	

	S	M	T	W	T	F	S
							1
D	2	3	4	5	6	7	8
E	9	10	11	12	13	14	15
C	16	17	18	19	20	21	22
	23	24	25	26	27	28	29
	30	31					

WEEKLY FOOD DIARY

	MONDAY	TUESDAY	WEDNESDAY	THURSDAY	FRIDAY	SATURDAY	SUNDAY
DAILY TOTALS	FRUIT ___ VEG ___ FAT ___ PROTEIN ___ BREAD ___ MILK ___ FLOATING ___	FRUIT ___ VEG ___ FAT ___ PROTEIN ___ BREAD ___ MILK ___ FLOATING ___	FRUIT ___ VEG ___ FAT ___ PROTEIN ___ BREAD ___ MILK ___ FLOATING ___	FRUIT ___ VEG ___ FAT ___ PROTEIN ___ BREAD ___ MILK ___ FLOATING ___	FRUIT ___ VEG ___ FAT ___ PROTEIN ___ BREAD ___ MILK ___ FLOATING ___	FRUIT ___ VEG ___ FAT ___ PROTEIN ___ BREAD ___ MILK ___ FLOATING ___	FRUIT ___ VEG ___ FAT ___ PROTEIN ___ BREAD ___ MILK ___ FLOATING ___
BREAKFAST							
LUNCH							
DINNER							
SNACKS							

WEEKLY LIMITS   EGGS ___   CHEESE ___   MEAT ___   ORGAN MEAT ___   OPTIONAL CALORIES ___

I will attend my Weight Watchers meeting this week on ___

NOVEMBER

DECEMBER

1 9 9 0

MONDAY
26

TUESDAY
27

WEDNESDAY
28

THURSDAY
29

FRIDAY
30

SATURDAY
1

SUNDAY
2

	S	M	T	W	T	F	S
			1	2	3	4	5	6
O	7	8	9	10	11	12	13
C	14	15	16	17	18	19	20
T	21	22	23	24	25	26	27
	28	29	30	31			

	S	M	T	W	T	F	S
					1	2	3
N	4	5	6	7	8	9	10
O	11	12	13	14	15	16	17
V	18	19	20	21	22	23	24
	25	26	27	28	29	30	

	S	M	T	W	T	F	S
							1
D	2	3	4	5	6	7	8
E	9	10	11	12	13	14	15
C	16	17	18	19	20	21	22
	23	24	25	26	27	28	29
	30	31					

WEIGHT
RECIPE
WATCHERS

Glazed Onions

Makes 2 servings, about 1 cup each

Water
2 cups pearl onions, peeled
1 tablespoon whipped butter

1 teaspoon *each* firmly packed brown
   sugar and light corn syrup
½ teaspoon molasses

Microwave Method: Set microwavable steamer insert in 1½-quart microwavable casserole; add ½ cup water (water should not touch insert). Arrange onions in insert, cover, and microwave on High (100%) for 4 minutes until onions are tender; set aside. In microwavable cup or small bowl combine remaining ingredients and microwave on High for 1 minute, until mixture begins to bubble.

    To serve, transfer onions to serving bowl; top with butter mixture and stir to coat.

Conventional Method: Set steamer insert in 1½-quart saucepan; add 1½ cups water (water should not touch insert). Arrange onions in insert, cover, and bring to a boil. Cook until onions are tender-crisp, 6 to 7 minutes.

    While onions are steaming, prepare butter mixture. In small saucepan combine remaining ingredients; cook over medium-high heat, stirring constantly with a wire whisk, until mixture comes to a boil, 2 to 3 minutes.

    To serve, transfer onions to serving bowl; top with butter mixture and stir to coat.

Each serving provides: 2 Vegetable Exchanges; 50 Optional Calories

Per serving: 115 calories; 2 g protein; 3 g fat; 22 g carbohydrate; 75 mg calcium; 50 mg sodium; 8 mg cholesterol; 0 g dietary fiber

Acorn Squash and Cheddar Gratin

Makes 2 servings

1 cooked acorn squash (about 1 pound), cut in half crosswise and seeded
1 small Red Delicious apple (about ¼ pound), cored and diced
¼ cup diced onion

1 tablespoon maple syrup
2 teaspoons freshly squeezed lemon juice
1 ounce sharp Cheddar cheese, shredded

Microwave Method: Cut a thin slice from the bottom of each squash half so halves stand upright. Using a spoon, scoop pulp from each squash half into a medium mixing bowl, leaving ¼-inch-thick shells; reserve shells. Mash pulp until smooth; set aside.

In 1-quart microwavable casserole combine apple, onion, syrup, and lemon juice and stir to combine; cover with vented plastic wrap and microwave on High (100%) for 2 minutes. Add apple mixture and cheese to squash pulp and mix until thoroughly combined. Spoon half of squash mixture into each reserved shell and set halves upright in casserole. Microwave on High for 2 minutes until cheese is melted.

Conventional Method: Cut a thin slice from the bottom of each squash half so halves stand upright. Using a spoon, scoop pulp from each squash half into a medium mixing bowl, leaving ¼-inch-thick shells; reserve shells. Mash pulp until smooth; set aside.

Preheat oven to 450°F. Spray 10-inch nonstick skillet with nonstick cooking spray and heat over medium-high heat; add apple and onion and sauté until onion is softened, about 1 minute. Add syrup and lemon juice and continue cooking, stirring occasionally, until apple is tender, 2 to 3 minutes. Add apple mixture and cheese to squash pulp and mix until thoroughly combined. Spoon half of squash mixture into each reserved shell and set halves upright in 1-quart casserole. Bake until cheese melts, about 5 minutes.

Each serving provides: ½ Protein Exchange; 2 Bread Exchanges; ¼ Vegetable Exchange; ½ Fruit Exchange; 30 Optional Calories

Per serving: 190 calories; 5 g protein; 5 g fat; 34 g carbohydrate; 178 mg calcium; 94 mg sodium; 15 mg cholesterol; 7 g dietary fiber

WEIGHT
RECIPE
WATCHERS

Turkey-Rice Dinner

Makes 2 servings

½ cup *each* sliced carrot, sliced mushrooms, and diced onion
2 teaspoons margarine
1 small garlic clove, minced
1½ cups water
2 ounces uncooked instant rice

1 packet instant chicken broth and seasoning mix
1 teaspoon browning sauce
¼ pound skinned and boned cooked turkey, cubed

Microwave Method: In 1-quart microwavable casserole combine vegetables, margarine, and garlic; stir well to thoroughly combine. Cover with vented plastic wrap and microwave on High (100%) for 2 minutes. Add remaining ingredients except turkey and stir to combine. Cover with vented plastic wrap and microwave on High for 8 minutes until rice is tender, stirring once halfway through cooking. Add turkey and stir to combine. Microwave on High for 2 minutes until heated through. Let stand for 2 minutes.

Conventional Method: In 10-inch nonstick skillet melt margarine; add vegetables and garlic and sauté over medium-high heat, stirring frequently, until vegetables are tender, 6 to 8 minutes. Add remaining ingredients except turkey; stir to combine and bring mixture to a boil. Reduce heat to low, cover, and let simmer until rice is tender and flavors blend, about 15 minutes. Add turkey and stir to combine; cook until heated through, about 5 minutes longer.

Each serving provides: 2 Protein Exchanges; 1 Bread Exchange; 1½ Vegetable Exchanges; 1 Fat Exchange; 5 Optional Calories

Per serving: 278 calories; 21 g protein; 7 g fat; 32 g carbohydrate; 39 mg calcium; 616 mg sodium; 44 mg cholesterol; 1 g dietary fiber (this figure does not include instant rice; nutrition analysis not available)

Spiced Poached Pear

Makes 2 servings

10 ounces pears, cored, pared, and cut lengthwise into ¼-inch-thick slices
⅓ cup dry white table wine
1 tablespoon honey

2 teaspoons lemon juice
2 whole cloves
One 2-inch cinnamon stick
1-inch piece pared gingerroot

Microwave Method: In 1-quart microwavable casserole combine all ingredients. Cover with vented plastic wrap and microwave on High (100%) for 3 minutes. Let stand, covered, for 2 minutes. Serve warm or refrigerate until chilled. Remove and discard cloves, cinnamon stick, and gingerroot just before serving.

Conventional Method: In 1-quart saucepan combine wine, honey, lemon juice, cloves, cinnamon stick, and gingerroot and stir until thoroughly combined; add pear slices and cook over medium-high heat until mixture comes to a boil. Reduce heat to low and let simmer until pears are tender, about 10 minutes. Serve warm or transfer to bowl, cover, and refrigerate until chilled. Remove and discard cloves, cinnamon stick, and gingerroot just before serving.

Each serving provides: 1 Fruit Exchange; 70 Optional Calories

Per serving: 139 calories; 1 g protein; 1 g fat; 30 g carbohydrate; 26 mg calcium; 4 mg sodium; 0 mg cholesterol; 3 g dietary fiber

DECEMBER

SUNDAY	MONDAY	TUESDAY	WEDNESDAY
2	3	4	5
9	10	11	12
16	17	18	19
23 / 30	24 / 31	25	26

DECEMBER

THURSDAY	FRIDAY	SATURDAY
		1
6	7	8
13	14	15
20	21	22
27	28	29

Microwave Menu of the Month

Roast Beef

Parslied Red Potatoes with Margarine

Cooked Broccoli Spears

Red and Green Leaf Lettuce Salad with Balsamic Vinegar and Herbs

Angel Food Cake drizzled with Chocolate Syrup

Fruity Rum Toddy

NOTES/GOALS

WEEKLY FOOD DIARY

	MONDAY	TUESDAY	WEDNESDAY	THURSDAY	FRIDAY	SATURDAY	SUNDAY
DAILY TOTALS	FRUIT ___ VEG ___ FAT ___ PROTEIN ___ BREAD ___ MILK ___ FLOATING ___	FRUIT ___ VEG ___ FAT ___ PROTEIN ___ BREAD ___ MILK ___ FLOATING ___	FRUIT ___ VEG ___ FAT ___ PROTEIN ___ BREAD ___ MILK ___ FLOATING ___	FRUIT ___ VEG ___ FAT ___ PROTEIN ___ BREAD ___ MILK ___ FLOATING ___	FRUIT ___ VEG ___ FAT ___ PROTEIN ___ BREAD ___ MILK ___ FLOATING ___	FRUIT ___ VEG ___ FAT ___ PROTEIN ___ BREAD ___ MILK ___ FLOATING ___	FRUIT ___ VEG ___ FAT ___ PROTEIN ___ BREAD ___ MILK ___ FLOATING ___
BREAKFAST							
LUNCH							
DINNER							
SNACKS							

WEEKLY LIMITS EGGS ___   CHEESE ___   MEAT ___   ORGAN MEAT ___   OPTIONAL CALORIES ___

I will attend my Weight Watchers meeting this week on ___

ENGAGEMENTS

DECEMBER

1990

MONDAY
3

TUESDAY
4

WEDNESDAY
5

THURSDAY
6

FRIDAY
7

SATURDAY
8

SUNDAY
9

	S	M	T	W	T	F	S
						1	2	3
N	4	5	6	7	8	9	10
O	11	12	13	14	15	16	17
V	18	19	20	21	22	23	24
	25	26	27	28	29	30	

	S	M	T	W	T	F	S
							1
D	2	3	4	5	6	7	8
E	9	10	11	12	13	14	15
C	16	17	18	19	20	21	22
	23	24	25	26	27	28	29
	30	31					

	S	M	T	W	T	F	S
		1	2	3	4	5
J	6	7	8	9	10	11	12
A	13	14	15	16	17	18	19
N	20	21	22	23	24	25	26
	27	28	29	30	31		

WEEKLY FOOD DIARY

	MONDAY	TUESDAY	WEDNESDAY	THURSDAY	FRIDAY	SATURDAY	SUNDAY
DAILY TOTALS	FRUIT ___ VEG ___ FAT ___ PROTEIN ___ BREAD ___ MILK ___ FLOATING ___	FRUIT ___ VEG ___ FAT ___ PROTEIN ___ BREAD ___ MILK ___ FLOATING ___	FRUIT ___ VEG ___ FAT ___ PROTEIN ___ BREAD ___ MILK ___ FLOATING ___	FRUIT ___ VEG ___ FAT ___ PROTEIN ___ BREAD ___ MILK ___ FLOATING ___	FRUIT ___ VEG ___ FAT ___ PROTEIN ___ BREAD ___ MILK ___ FLOATING ___	FRUIT ___ VEG ___ FAT ___ PROTEIN ___ BREAD ___ MILK ___ FLOATING ___	FRUIT ___ VEG ___ FAT ___ PROTEIN ___ BREAD ___ MILK ___ FLOATING ___
BREAKFAST							
LUNCH							
DINNER							
SNACKS							

WEEKLY LIMITS EGGS _____ CHEESE _____ MEAT _____ ORGAN MEAT _____ OPTIONAL CALORIES _____

I will attend my Weight Watchers meeting this week on _____

ENGAGEMENTS

DECEMBER

1 9 9 0

MONDAY
10

TUESDAY
11

First Day of Hanukkah

WEDNESDAY
12

THURSDAY
13

FRIDAY
14

SATURDAY
15

SUNDAY
16

	S	M	T	W	T	F	S
					1	2	3
N	4	5	6	7	8	9	10
O	11	12	13	14	15	16	17
V	18	19	20	21	22	23	24
	25	26	27	28	29	30	

	S	M	T	W	T	F	S
							1
D	2	3	4	5	6	7	8
E	9	10	11	12	13	14	15
C	16	17	18	19	20	21	22
	23	24	25	26	27	28	29
	30	31					

	S	M	T	W	T	F	S
		1	2	3	4	5	
J	6	7	8	9	10	11	12
A	13	14	15	16	17	18	19
N	20	21	22	23	24	25	26
	27	28	29	30	31		

WEEKLY FOOD DIARY

	MONDAY	TUESDAY	WEDNESDAY	THURSDAY	FRIDAY	SATURDAY	SUNDAY
DAILY TOTALS	FRUIT ____ VEG ____ FAT ____ PROTEIN ____ BREAD ____ MILK ____ FLOATING ____	FRUIT ____ VEG ____ FAT ____ PROTEIN ____ BREAD ____ MILK ____ FLOATING ____	FRUIT ____ VEG ____ FAT ____ PROTEIN ____ BREAD ____ MILK ____ FLOATING ____	FRUIT ____ VEG ____ FAT ____ PROTEIN ____ BREAD ____ MILK ____ FLOATING ____	FRUIT ____ VEG ____ FAT ____ PROTEIN ____ BREAD ____ MILK ____ FLOATING ____	FRUIT ____ VEG ____ FAT ____ PROTEIN ____ BREAD ____ MILK ____ FLOATING ____	FRUIT ____ VEG ____ FAT ____ PROTEIN ____ BREAD ____ MILK ____ FLOATING ____
BREAKFAST							
LUNCH							
DINNER							
SNACKS							

WEEKLY LIMITS   EGGS ____   CHEESE ____   MEAT ____   ORGAN MEAT ____   OPTIONAL CALORIES ____

I will attend my Weight Watchers meeting this week on _____

DECEMBER

1990

MONDAY
17

TUESDAY
18

WEDNESDAY
19

THURSDAY
20

FRIDAY
21

SATURDAY
22

SUNDAY
23

	S	M	T	W	T	F	S
						1	2	3
N	4	5	6	7	8	9	10
O	11	12	13	14	15	16	17
V	18	19	20	21	22	23	24
	25	26	27	28	29	30	

	S	M	T	W	T	F	S
							1
D	2	3	4	5	6	7	8
E	9	10	11	12	13	14	15
C	16	17	18	19	20	21	22
	23	24	25	26	27	28	29
	30	31					

	S	M	T	W	T	F	S
		1	2	3	4	5
J	6	7	8	9	10	11	12
A	13	14	15	16	17	18	19
N	20	21	22	23	24	25	26
	27	28	29	30	31		

WEEKLY FOOD DIARY

	MONDAY	TUESDAY	WEDNESDAY	THURSDAY	FRIDAY	SATURDAY	SUNDAY
D A I L Y T O T A L S	FRUIT ____ VEG ____ FAT ____ PROTEIN ____ BREAD ____ MILK ____ FLOATING ____	FRUIT ____ VEG ____ FAT ____ PROTEIN ____ BREAD ____ MILK ____ FLOATING ____	FRUIT ____ VEG ____ FAT ____ PROTEIN ____ BREAD ____ MILK ____ FLOATING ____	FRUIT ____ VEG ____ FAT ____ PROTEIN ____ BREAD ____ MILK ____ FLOATING ____	FRUIT ____ VEG ____ FAT ____ PROTEIN ____ BREAD ____ MILK ____ FLOATING ____	FRUIT ____ VEG ____ FAT ____ PROTEIN ____ BREAD ____ MILK ____ FLOATING ____	FRUIT ____ VEG ____ FAT ____ PROTEIN ____ BREAD ____ MILK ____ FLOATING ____
B R E A K F A S T							
L U N C H							
D I N N E R							
S N A C K S							

WEEKLY LIMITS   EGGS ____   CHEESE ____   MEAT ____   ORGAN MEAT ____   OPTIONAL CALORIES ____

I will attend my Weight Watchers meeting this week on ____

DECEMBER

MONDAY
24

Christmas Day

TUESDAY
25

Boxing Day (Canada)

WEDNESDAY
26

THURSDAY
27

FRIDAY
28

SATURDAY
29

SUNDAY
30

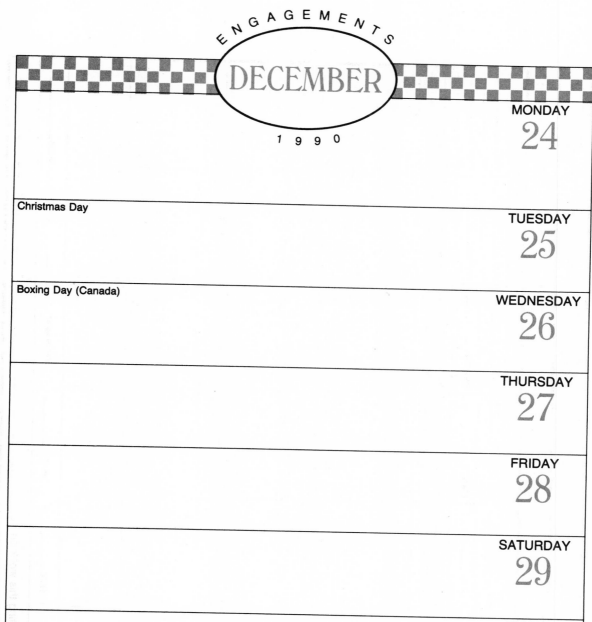

	S	M	T	W	T	F	S
					1	2	3
N	4	5	6	7	8	9	10
O	11	12	13	14	15	16	17
V	18	19	20	21	22	23	24
	25	26	27	28	29	30	

	S	M	T	W	T	F	S
							1
D	2	3	4	5	6	7	8
E	9	10	11	12	13	14	15
C	16	17	18	19	20	21	22
	23	24	25	26	27	28	29
	30	31					

	S	M	T	W	T	F	S
			1	2	3	4	5
J	6	7	8	9	10	11	12
A	13	14	15	16	17	18	19
N	20	21	22	23	24	25	26
	27	28	29	30	31		

WEEKLY FOOD DIARY

	MONDAY	TUESDAY	WEDNESDAY	THURSDAY	FRIDAY	SATURDAY	SUNDAY
DAILY TOTALS	FRUIT ___ VEG ___ FAT ___ PROTEIN ___ BREAD ___ MILK ___ FLOATING ___	FRUIT ___ VEG ___ FAT ___ PROTEIN ___ BREAD ___ MILK ___ FLOATING ___	FRUIT ___ VEG ___ FAT ___ PROTEIN ___ BREAD ___ MILK ___ FLOATING ___	FRUIT ___ VEG ___ FAT ___ PROTEIN ___ BREAD ___ MILK ___ FLOATING ___	FRUIT ___ VEG ___ FAT ___ PROTEIN ___ BREAD ___ MILK ___ FLOATING ___	FRUIT ___ VEG ___ FAT ___ PROTEIN ___ BREAD ___ MILK ___ FLOATING ___	FRUIT ___ VEG ___ FAT ___ PROTEIN ___ BREAD ___ MILK ___ FLOATING ___
BREAKFAST							
LUNCH							
DINNER							
SNACKS							

WEEKLY LIMITS   EGGS ___   CHEESE ___   MEAT ___   ORGAN MEAT ___   OPTIONAL CALORIES ___

I will attend my Weight Watchers meeting this week on _____

DECEMBER
JANUARY

1 9 9 0

New Year's Eve 1990

MONDAY
31

New Year's Day 1991

TUESDAY
1

WEDNESDAY
2

THURSDAY
3

FRIDAY
4

SATURDAY
5

SUNDAY
6

	S	M	T	W	T	F	S
					1	2	3
N	4	5	6	7	8	9	10
O	11	12	13	14	15	16	17
V	18	19	20	21	22	23	24
	25	26	27	28	29	30	

	S	M	T	W	T	F	S
							1
D	2	3	4	5	6	7	8
E	9	10	11	12	13	14	15
C	16	17	18	19	20	21	22
	23	24	25	26	27	28	29
	30	31					

	S	M	T	W	T	F	S
			1	2	3	4	5
J	6	7	8	9	10	11	12
A	13	14	15	16	17	18	19
N	20	21	22	23	24	25	26
	27	28	29	30	31		

Stuffed Mushrooms

Makes 2 servings, 4 mushrooms each

8 large mushrooms (2-inch diameter each)
1 tablespoon chopped scallion (green onion), green and white portion

1 teaspoon margarine
1 ounce Swiss cheese, shredded
½ ounce seasoned croutons
Dash Italian seasoning

Microwave Method: Remove stems from mushrooms; mince stems, reserving caps. In small microwavable mixing bowl combine mushroom stems, scallion, and margarine; stir well to thoroughly combine. Microwave on High (100%) for 1 minute; add remaining ingredients except mushroom caps and stir to combine.

Fill each mushroom cap with an equal amount of cheese mixture and arrange in a circle around outer edge of microwavable plate. Microwave on High for 2 minutes, rotating each mushroom ½ turn halfway through cooking, until cheese is melted.

Conventional Method: Remove stems from mushrooms; mince stems, reserving caps. In small nonstick skillet melt margarine; add mushroom stems and scallion and sauté over medium heat until softened, about 2 minutes. Remove from heat; add remaining ingredients except mushroom caps and stir to combine.

Fill each mushroom cap with an equal amount of cheese mixture and arrange on nonstick baking sheet. Broil 6 inches from heat source until cheese is melted and lightly browned, 2 to 3 minutes.

Each serving provides: ½ Protein Exchange; ½ Bread Exchange; 2¾ Vegetable Exchanges; ½ Fat Exchange

Per serving: 109 calories; 7 g protein; 7 g fat; 7 g carbohydrate; 145 mg calcium; 86 mg sodium; 13 mg cholesterol; 3 g dietary fiber

Zucchini Boats with Veal Stuffing

Makes 2 servings

1 large zucchini (about 10 ounces)
¼ cup *each* minced red onion, celery, and carrot
1 teaspoon olive *or* vegetable oil
1 garlic clove, minced
5 ounces ground veal
3 tablespoons plain dried bread crumbs

1 egg white
1 tablespoon minced Italian (flat-leaf) parsley
⅛ teaspoon *each* rubbed sage, thyme leaves, and salt
½ cup tomato sauce
1 tablespoon grated Parmesan cheese

Microwave Method: Cut zucchini in half lengthwise and remove pulp, leaving ½-inch-thick shells; chop pulp.

In medium microwavable mixing bowl combine zucchini pulp, vegetables, oil, and garlic; stir well to thoroughly combine. Microwave on High (100%) for 3 minutes; let cool slightly. Add remaining ingredients except tomato sauce and cheese and stir to combine.

Spoon half of veal mixture into each zucchini shell; set zucchini in 12 × 8-inch microwavable baking dish. Top each shell with half of the tomato sauce and cheese. Cover with vented plastic wrap and microwave on High for 7 minutes until veal is no longer pink, rotating dish ½ turn halfway through cooking. Let stand for 2 minutes.

Conventional Method: Prepare zucchini as directed in microwave method. In 10-inch nonstick skillet heat oil; add zucchini pulp, vegetables, and garlic and sauté over medium-high heat until vegetables are tender-crisp, about 2 minutes. Transfer to medium mixing bowl and let cool slightly; add remaining ingredients except tomato sauce and cheese and stir to combine.

Preheat oven to 375°F. Fill zucchini shells as directed in microwave method. Set zucchini in 12 × 8-inch baking dish. Top each shell with half of the tomato sauce and cheese. Bake until veal is no longer pink, about 35 minutes.

Each serving provides: 2 Protein Exchanges; ½ Bread Exchange; 3¼ Vegetable Exchanges; ½ Fat Exchange; 25 Optional Calories

Per serving: 257 calories; 21 g protein; 11 g fat; 20 g carbohydrate; 109 mg calcium; 721 mg sodium; 53 mg cholesterol; 2 g dietary fiber

WEIGHT
RECIPE
WATCHERS

Cheesecake Cups

Makes 4 servings

1 cup cottage cheese
⅓ cup plus 2 teaspoons whipped cream
  cheese
1 egg

1 tablespoon granulated sugar
½ teaspoon vanilla extract
2 graham crackers (2½-inch squares),
  made into crumbs

Microwave Method: In blender container combine all ingredients except crumbs and process until smooth. Spray four 6-ounce microwavable custard cups with nonstick cooking spray and spoon ¼ of cheese mixture into each cup; sprinkle each with ¼ of the crumbs. Microwave on Medium (50%) for 8 minutes, rotating each cup ½ turn halfway through cooking. Let stand for 1 minute.

Conventional Method: Preheat oven to 350°F. In blender container combine all ingredients except crumbs and process until smooth. Spray four 6-ounce custard cups with nonstick cooking spray and spoon ¼ of cheese mixture into each cup; sprinkle each with ¼ of the crumbs. Set cups on baking sheet and bake until cheese mixture is set and crumb mixture is golden brown, about 20 minutes.

Each serving provides: 1 Protein Exchange; ¼ Bread Exchange; 65 Optional Calories

Per serving: 149 calories; 9 g protein; 9 g fat; 8 g carbohydrate; 49 mg calcium; 306 mg sodium; 91 mg cholesterol; 0.4 g dietary fiber

WEIGHT
RECIPE
WATCHERS

Fruity Rum Toddy

Makes 2 servings, about ¾ cup each

1 cup water
One 2-inch cinnamon stick
10 whole cloves
2 tea bags

2 lemon wedges
⅓ cup *each* apricot nectar and
pineapple juice (no sugar added)
1 tablespoon dark rum

Microwave Method: In small microwavable mixing bowl combine water, cinnamon stick, and 4 cloves; microwave on High (100%) for 3 minutes until water comes to a full boil. Add tea bags and let stand for 3 minutes or until desired strength.

Insert 3 of the remaining cloves into peel of each lemon wedge; set aside. Remove and discard tea bags and spices; stir in nectar, juice, and rum. Microwave on High for 30 seconds until thoroughly heated. Divide into two 8-ounce mugs; set 1 lemon wedge on rim of each mug.

Conventional Method: In small saucepan combine water, cinnamon stick, and 4 cloves and cook over high heat until mixture comes to a full boil. Remove from heat; add tea bags and let stand for 3 minutes or until desired strength.

Insert 3 of the remaining cloves into peel of each lemon wedge; set aside. Remove and discard tea bags and spices; stir in nectar, juice, and rum. Cook over low heat until mixture begins to simmer and is thoroughly heated. Divide into two 8-ounce mugs; set 1 lemon wedge on rim of each mug.

Each serving provides: 1 Fruit Exchange; 20 Optional Calories

Per serving: 71 calories; 0.5 g protein; 0.2 g fat; 15 g carbohydrate; 34 mg calcium; 10 mg sodium; 0 mg cholesterol; 0.1 g dietary fiber

Microwave Know-How

Vegetables: Specialties of the Microwave

Crisp, colorful, flavorful, and nutritious . . . that's how vegetables cook up in the microwave oven. It's the quick cooking using little or no water that makes the microwave perfect for vegetables. For best results, keep in mind the following hints:

• Smaller pieces of vegetables will cook more evenly and in less time than larger pieces. For even cooking, keep pieces uniform in size and thickness.

• If large vegetables are cooked until the center is tender, the outer portions will become mushy. When cooking larger vegetables, be sure to allow for standing time. Standing time permits vegetables to become tender without losing texture.

• The quantity of vegetables you are cooking will influence the cooking time. A small amount will cook in less time than a large amount.

• Chilled vegetables will take slightly longer to cook than those at room temperature.

• The moisture content and maturity of a vegetable will also affect the cooking time. Since younger vegetables are moister than those that are harvested late in the season, they will cook in less time and need less water.

• Broccoli and asparagus spears require special attention because their stems as not as tender as the tops. To insure even cooking, arrange them in a baking dish with the stems at the outer edge of the dish and the tender tops in the center.

• Pierce or cut vegetables to be cooked in their skins, such as winter squash and potatoes, prior to cooking in the microwave oven. This allows excess steam to escape, which will prevent bursting.

• When cooking several large vegetables, such as winter squash or potatoes, arrange them in a ring in a baking dish or on the oven floor, leaving the center open and a space between each vegetable. For even cooking, rotate both the vegetables and the baking dish halfway through the cooking process.

• Cover vegetables to retain moisture and speed cooking. Use a casserole with a matching cover or vented plastic wrap. Whole skinless vegetables, such as husked corn on the cob or an artichoke, can be wrapped in plastic wrap or wax paper and cooked without a casserole.

• Stir small pieces of vegetables halfway through cooking from the outside of the dish to the center to distribute heat evenly.

The microwave oven is the key to faster meal preparation, as you'll discover when you follow our steps for preparing these versatile foods.

Speedy Squash—Acorn squash bakes in practically no time in the microwave oven. To cook a one-pound acorn squash, cut it in half crosswise, then remove and discard the seeds. Place squash halves cut-side down in a microwavable 8 × 8 × 2-inch baking dish. Cover with vented plastic wrap and cook on High (100%) for 5 minutes until squash is fork-tender, rotating the dish ½ turn halfway through cooking.

Beat-the-Clock Baked Potatoes—Why wait an hour for baked potatoes to cook in a conventional oven? In the microwave, a whole potato will cook in less time than potato slices because the skin helps to hold in steam and heat. To cook, pierce a 6-ounce potato with a fork, then place the potato on a sheet of paper towel on the floor of the oven. Microwave for 4 to 6 minutes, turning the potato over halfway through cooking. Let stand to soften.

Quick Corn on the Cob with that Just-Picked Taste—Corn on the cob can be microwaved in the husk or without the husk. To cook 2 small ears of corn on the cob in the husk, place corn on the floor of the oven, leaving space between the ears. Microwave for 4 to 5 minutes, turning corn halfway through cooking. To remove the husk, wrap the base end of the corn with paper towel and, holding the towel-covered base, fold back the leaves of the husk, being careful of hot steam. Pull out corn silk and remove the husk.

There are two ways to microwave husked corn. One is to place both ears of corn in an 8 × 8 × 2-inch microwavable baking dish along with ¼ cup water, leaving space between the ears. Cover the baking dish with vented plastic wrap and cook for 5 to 6 minutes, turning the dish ¼ turn every 2 minutes.

The second method for cooking husked corn will save you the trouble of having a baking dish to wash. Wrap each ear of corn individually in plastic wrap or wax paper and place on the floor of the oven. Microwave for 5 to 6 minutes, turning the corn halfway through cooking.

Crisp Bacon with No Messy Skillet to Clean!—Bacon cooked in the microwave needs less attention than pan-fried bacon. There's no need to turn slices over or drain off excess grease. To cook 2 slices of bacon, arrange slices in a single layer on a microwavable roasting rack or on a microwavable plate lined with three layers of paper towel. Cover with paper towel to prevent spattering and microwave on High (100%) for 1 to 2 minutes. For crisper bacon, let stand for 1 to 2 minutes.

Reheat Pasta and Rice in a Jiffy—In a 1-quart microwavable bowl arrange 1 cup cooked pasta or rice. Cover with wax paper and microwave on High (100%) for 1 to 2 minutes.

Instant rice cooks perfectly in the microwave oven. Measure 4 ounces instant rice and set in a 1½-quart microwavable bowl; stir in 1 cup hot tap water. Cover with vented plastic wrap and microwave on High (100%) for 10 minutes. Drain and serve.

Although pasta can be cooked in the microwave oven with satisfactory results, it will take about as much time as pasta cooked in a saucepan on top of the range. An easy way to save time in the kitchen is to use *both* appliances. While the pasta is cooking on the range, you can use your microwave for preparing the other steps in the recipe.

Toast Coconut in Seconds—Toasted, shredded coconut adds a tropical touch to familiar treats. To toast coconut in the microwave, spread 1 table-spoon coconut evenly on a glass plate and microwave on High (100%) for 40 to 50 seconds, checking and stirring every 20 seconds. Sprinkle it over fresh fruit salad, reduced-calorie gelatin or pudding, ice milk or ice cream.

The One-Bowl Scrambled Egg—In small microwavable bowl microwave ½ teaspoon margarine on High (100%) for 10 seconds, until melted. Add egg and 2 tablespoons skim, low-fat, or whole milk (or water) and beat with a fork until combined. Microwave partially covered for 1 minute on Medium-High (70%); stir and continue to cook on Medium-High, partially covered, until almost set, ½ to 1 minute. Let stand ½ to 1 minute before serving.

Melt It in the Microwave—Double boilers for melting chocolate, margarine, or butter are a thing of the past. When you use the microwave, you don't need to cook the food until it melts completely; you can stir the last few unmelted pieces into the already-melted mixture.

Gelatin Gems—Your microwave oven can speed the process of dissolving gelatin. In small microwavable bowl measure water as directed on package and microwave on High (100%) for 2 to 3 minutes until boiling. Add gelatin and stir until dissolved. Stir in cold water or ice cubes. If the gelatin has set before you've added other ingredients (fruit, vegetables, or nuts), you can soften the gelatin in the microwave on Medium (50%), for 1 to 1½ minutes for a 3-ounce package of prepared gelatin, and 1 to 2 minutes for a 6-ounce package. Stir in the additional ingredients and pop the gelatin mixture back in the refrigerator until it is firm.

Look What's Popping Up—You know about microwave popcorn no doubt, but did you know that you can also reheat cold popcorn? For each cup of prepared popcorn, microwave on High (100%) for 15 to 20 seconds to bring back that delicious, just-popped flavor.

Viva Vegetables for One—For a serving of vegetables in a flash, just com-bine ½ cup frozen vegetables and 1 tablespoon water in 10-ounce micro-wavable custard cup and cover with wax paper. Microwave on High (100%) for 1½ to 2 minutes.

Just Dandy Dried Fruit—For perfectly plump dried fruit, arrange fruit in 6-ounce microwavable custard cup, sprinkle with a small amount of water, and microwave on High (100%) for 15 to 30 seconds.

Juicier Lemons and Limes—Want to get more juice out of lemons, limes, or oranges? Microwave on High (100%) for 15 to 30 seconds before squeezing.

Here's the Scoop—To soften up a solid block of ice milk or ice cream, put the container in the microwave on Low (20%) for about 45 seconds. Scooping will be much easier.

Weight Watchers Metric Conversion Table

WEIGHT

To Change	To	Multiply by
Ounces	Grams	30.0
Pounds	Kilograms	0.48

VOLUME

To Change	To	Multiply by
Teaspoons	Milliliters	5.0
Tablespoons	Milliliters	15.0
Cups	Milliliters	250.0
Cups	Liters	0.25
Pints	Liters	0.5
Quarts	Liters	1.0
Gallons	Liters	4.0

LENGTH

To Change	To	Multiply by
Inches	Millimeters	25.0
Inches	Centimeters	2.5
Feet	Centimeters	30.0
Yards	Meters	0.9

TEMPERATURE

To change degrees Fahrenheit to degrees Celsius subtract 32° and multiply by $\frac{5}{9}$.

Oven Temperatures

Degrees Fahrenheit	= Degrees Celsius	Degrees Fahrenheit	= Degrees Celsius
250	120	400	200
275	140	425	220
300	150	450	230
325	160	475	250
350	180	500	260
375	190	525	270

METRIC SYMBOLS

Symbol	= Metric Unit	Symbol	= Metric Unit
g	gram	°C	degrees Celsius
kg	kilogram	mm	millimeter
ml	milliliter	cm	centimeter
l	liter	m	meter

Dry and Liquid Measure Equivalents

Teaspoons	Tablespoons	Cups	Fluid Ounces
			½ fluid ounce
3 teaspoons	1 tablespoon		1 fluid ounce
6 teaspoons	2 tablespoons	⅛ cup	2 fluid ounces
12 teaspoons	4 tablespoons	¼ cup	
16 teaspoons	5 tablespoons plus 1 teaspoon	⅓ cup	
18 teaspoons	6 tablespoons	⅓ cup plus 2 teaspoons	3 fluid ounces
24 teaspoons	8 tablespoons	½ cup	4 fluid ounces
30 teaspoons	10 tablespoons	½ cup plus 2 tablespoons	5 fluid ounces
32 teaspoons	10 tablespoons plus 2 teaspoons	⅔ cup	
36 teaspoons	12 tablespoons	¾ cup	6 fluid ounces
42 teaspoons	14 tablespoons	1 cup less 2 tablespoons	7 fluid ounces
48 teaspoons	16 tablespoons	1 cup	8 fluid ounces
96 teaspoons	32 tablespoons	2 cups (1 pint)	16 fluid ounces
		4 cups (1 quart)	32 fluid ounces

Note: Measurements of less than ⅛ teaspoon are considered a dash or a pinch.

INDEX

Each recipe in this ENGAGEMENT CALENDAR is listed alphabetically, followed by the month in which it is featured.

1989

JANUARY
S	M	T	W	T	F	S
1	2	3	4	5	6	7
8	9	10	11	12	13	14
15	16	17	18	19	20	21
22	23	24	25	26	27	28
29	30	31				

FEBRUARY
S	M	T	W	T	F	S
			1	2	3	4
5	6	7	8	9	10	11
12	13	14	15	16	17	18
19	20	21	22	23	24	25
26	27	28				

MARCH
S	M	T	W	T	F	S
			1	2	3	4
5	6	7	8	9	10	11
12	13	14	15	16	17	18
19	20	21	22	23	24	25
26	27	28	29	30	31	

APRIL
S	M	T	W	T	F	S
						1
2	3	4	5	6	7	8
9	10	11	12	13	14	15
16	17	18	19	20	21	22
23/30	24	25	26	27	28	29

MAY
S	M	T	W	T	F	S
	1	2	3	4	5	6
7	8	9	10	11	12	13
14	15	16	17	18	19	20
21	22	23	24	25	26	27
28	29	30	31			

JUNE
S	M	T	W	T	F	S
				1	2	3
4	5	6	7	8	9	10
11	12	13	14	15	16	17
18	19	20	21	22	23	24
25	26	27	28	29	30	

JULY
S	M	T	W	T	F	S
						1
2	3	4	5	6	7	8
9	10	11	12	13	14	15
16	17	18	19	20	21	22
23/30	24/31	25	26	27	28	29

AUGUST
S	M	T	W	T	F	S
		1	2	3	4	5
6	7	8	9	10	11	12
13	14	15	16	17	18	19
20	21	22	23	24	25	26
27	28	29	30	31		

SEPTEMBER
S	M	T	W	T	F	S
					1	2
3	4	5	6	7	8	9
10	11	12	13	14	15	16
17	18	19	20	21	22	23
24	25	26	27	28	29	30

OCTOBER
S	M	T	W	T	F	S
1	2	3	4	5	6	7
8	9	10	11	12	13	14
15	16	17	18	19	20	21
22	23	24	25	26	27	28
29	30	31				

NOVEMBER
S	M	T	W	T	F	S
			1	2	3	4
5	6	7	8	9	10	11
12	13	14	15	16	17	18
19	20	21	22	23	24	25
26	27	28	29	30		

DECEMBER
S	M	T	W	T	F	S
					1	2
3	4	5	6	7	8	9
10	11	12	13	14	15	16
17	18	19	20	21	22	23
24/31	25	26	27	28	29	30

1990

JANUARY
S	M	T	W	T	F	S
	1	2	3	4	5	6
7	8	9	10	11	12	13
14	15	16	17	18	19	20
21	22	23	24	25	26	27
28	29	30	31			

FEBRUARY
S	M	T	W	T	F	S
				1	2	3
4	5	6	7	8	9	10
11	12	13	14	15	16	17
18	19	20	21	22	23	24
25	26	27	28			

MARCH
S	M	T	W	T	F	S
				1	2	3
4	5	6	7	8	9	10
11	12	13	14	15	16	17
18	19	20	21	22	23	24
25	26	27	28	29	30	31

APRIL
S	M	T	W	T	F	S
1	2	3	4	5	6	7
8	9	10	11	12	13	14
15	16	17	18	19	20	21
22	23	24	25	26	27	28
29	30					

MAY
S	M	T	W	T	F	S
		1	2	3	4	5
6	7	8	9	10	11	12
13	14	15	16	17	18	19
20	21	22	23	24	25	26
27	28	29	30	31		

JUNE
S	M	T	W	T	F	S
					1	2
3	4	5	6	7	8	9
10	11	12	13	14	15	16
17	18	19	20	21	22	23
24	25	26	27	28	29	30

JULY
S	M	T	W	T	F	S
1	2	3	4	5	6	7
8	9	10	11	12	13	14
15	16	17	18	19	20	21
22	23	24	25	26	27	28
29	30	31				

AUGUST
S	M	T	W	T	F	S
			1	2	3	4
5	6	7	8	9	10	11
12	13	14	15	16	17	18
19	20	21	22	23	24	25
26	27	28	29	30	31	

SEPTEMBER
S	M	T	W	T	F	S
						1
2	3	4	5	6	7	8
9	10	11	12	13	14	15
16	17	18	19	20	21	22
23/30	24	25	26	27	28	29

OCTOBER
S	M	T	W	T	F	S
	1	2	3	4	5	6
7	8	9	10	11	12	13
14	15	16	17	18	19	20
21	22	23	24	25	26	27
28	29	30	31			

NOVEMBER
S	M	T	W	T	F	S
				1	2	3
4	5	6	7	8	9	10
11	12	13	14	15	16	17
18	19	20	21	22	23	24
25	26	27	28	29	30	

DECEMBER
S	M	T	W	T	F	S
						1
2	3	4	5	6	7	8
9	10	11	12	13	14	15
16	17	18	19	20	21	22
23/30	24/31	25	26	27	28	29

1991

JANUARY
S	M	T	W	T	F	S
		1	2	3	4	5
6	7	8	9	10	11	12
13	14	15	16	17	18	19
20	21	22	23	24	25	26
27	28	29	30	31		

FEBRUARY
S	M	T	W	T	F	S
					1	2
3	4	5	6	7	8	9
10	11	12	13	14	15	16
17	18	19	20	21	22	23
24	25	26	27	28		

MARCH
S	M	T	W	T	F	S
					1	2
3	4	5	6	7	8	9
10	11	12	13	14	15	16
17	18	19	20	21	22	23
24/31	25	26	27	28	29	30

APRIL
S	M	T	W	T	F	S
	1	2	3	4	5	6
7	8	9	10	11	12	13
14	15	16	17	18	19	20
21	22	23	24	25	26	27
28	29	30				

MAY
S	M	T	W	T	F	S
			1	2	3	4
5	6	7	8	9	10	11
12	13	14	15	16	17	18
19	20	21	22	23	24	25
26	27	28	29	30	31	

JUNE
S	M	T	W	T	F	S
						1
2	3	4	5	6	7	8
9	10	11	12	13	14	15
16	17	18	19	20	21	22
23/30	24	25	26	27	28	29

JULY
S	M	T	W	T	F	S
	1	2	3	4	5	6
7	8	9	10	11	12	13
14	15	16	17	18	19	20
21	22	23	24	25	26	27
28	29	30	31			

AUGUST
S	M	T	W	T	F	S
				1	2	3
4	5	6	7	8	9	10
11	12	13	14	15	16	17
18	19	20	21	22	23	24
25	26	27	28	29	30	31

SEPTEMBER
S	M	T	W	T	F	S
1	2	3	4	5	6	7
8	9	10	11	12	13	14
15	16	17	18	19	20	21
22	23	24	25	26	27	28
29	30					

OCTOBER
S	M	T	W	T	F	S
		1	2	3	4	5
6	7	8	9	10	11	12
13	14	15	16	17	18	19
20	21	22	23	24	25	26
27	28	29	30	31		

NOVEMBER
S	M	T	W	T	F	S
					1	2
3	4	5	6	7	8	9
10	11	12	13	14	15	16
17	18	19	20	21	22	23
24	25	26	27	28	29	30

DECEMBER
S	M	T	W	T	F	S
1	2	3	4	5	6	7
8	9	10	11	12	13	14
15	16	17	18	19	20	21
22	23	24	25	26	27	28
29	30	31				